SOMETHING INHUMAN
WALKED THE FOREST

An alien presence whose awesome potential rendered Steve Austin's superpowers useless.

It had been sent from outer space on a secret mission. A devastating experiment that threatened to reduce an entire state to rubble...

THE SECRET OF
BIGFOOT PASS

A NERVE-SIZZLING NOVEL STARRING
THE SIX MILLION DOLLAR MAN

Look for more of THE SIX MILLION DOLLAR MAN in

WELCOME HOME, JAIME

adventures of THE BIONIC WOMAN

THE SIX MILLION DOLLAR MAN

THE SECRET OF BIG FOOT PASS

Based on the Universal television series
Created by Martin Caidin
Adapted from the episodes written by Kenneth Johnson

A BERKLEY MEDALLION BOOK
published by
BERKLEY PUBLISHING CORPORATION

Published by arrangement with MCA Publishing

MCA Publishing
100 Universal City Plaza
Universal City, California 91608

SBN 425-03307-4

BERKLEY MEDALLION BOOKS are published by
Berkley Publishing Corporation
200 Madison Avenue
New York, N.Y. 10016

BERKLEY MEDALLION BOOK ® TM 757,375

Printed in the United States of America

Berkley Medallion Edition, OCTOBER, 1976

THE SIX MILLION DOLLAR MAN

THE SECRET OF BIGFOOT PASS

Chapter One

Ivan and Marlene Beckey didn't look like scientists, but then, scientists rarely do anymore. It was a long time since men of science were either doddering old white-haired men with Germanic accents or stiff, humorless young men with horn-rimmed glasses and hair slicked straight back. Both Ivan and Marlene Beckey were good-looking, in their early thirties, with long brown hair that looked unkempt. They preferred the field to the library, and spent as much time in it as possible. One day in June, a day that was very nearly their last, the field in which they worked was an old Indian trail running through the Salmon Mountains of northern California.

The Beckeys were geologists attached to the National Center for Earthquake Research in Menlo Park, California, the institute that took upon itself the responsibility of monitoring the quirks of the San Andreas Fault. That geological troublespot, which causes most of California's famous earthquakes, had a half-dozen minor faults running perpendicular to it. One of them, the Trinity Fault, was the discovery of Ivan and Marlene Beckey. It was the basis for their doctorates at Stanford, and it was the reason they were hiking through the Salmon-Trinity Alps Wilderness, looking very much like backpackers out for a casual weekend jaunt.

The coniferous forest was beautiful, uninhabited, and smelled of pine needles. To their right, Thompson Peak rose better than nine thousand feet into the air, its peak hidden from their view by thin clouds. A bit further to the northeast, Battle Mountain obscured a part of the horizon. Between the two peaks, South Fork Creek wound southward toward the hamlet of Trinity Center, near which the geological team backing up the Beckeys had established its base camp.

They crossed a small rivulet leading to South Fork Creek, hiked a few hundred yards further down the trail, and came to a small clearing. The clearing was on a slope, covered with native grass, and had a view of both Thompson Peak and Battle Mountain. The only sound was that made by an occasional western tanager and mourning dove. Ivan Beckey came to a halt, slipped his heavy blue backback from his shoulders, took a deep breath and sighed loudly.

"So this is the forest primeval," he said.

His wife smiled and eased her backpack to the ground.

"Very poetic," she said.

"Is it?" he said. "Actually, I get the feeling a troop of boy scouts is going to overrun us at any moment."

"Not a chance," she replied. "This whole area is forty miles east of nowhere. That's why no one ever noticed our fault before."

"Our fault," Ivan said, grabbing her from behind, "was not coming here before. How about a second honeymoon, right here? Like you said, there's nobody closer than forty miles."

"What about the boy scouts?" she asked.

"Forget 'em," he said. "They've become very broad-minded in recent years. They have merit badges in *everything*."

"Discipline, Dr. Beckey. You're here as a geologist, not a husband."

He frowned and let go of her.

"You're a slave driver, Dr. Beckey," he replied.

He bit her neck lightly and pouted playfully when she pulled away. Marlene bent over, unsnapped her backpack, and from the top compartment, withdrew a shiny steel cylinder about ten inches in length and five inches in breadth. While her husband watched, she screwed a base-loaded VHF telemetry antenna onto the top of the cylinder and a three-foot, stainless-steel probe onto the bottom.

"Do you really think these very expensive transistor radios are going to help predict earthquakes?" she asked.

"I certainly hope so," Ivan replied, working an adapted seed-drill to make a deep, narrow hole in the ground in which his wife would insert the probe. "If they don't, we sure wasted a lot of time planting twenty-two of them along the north end of the San Andreas Fault and eighteen of them along the Trinity Fault." Ivan grinned. "They work," he said, "and you know it."

The man completed digging the hole and pulled the adapted seed-drill from it. He shook the dirt onto the ground and watched as Marlene pushed the three-foot-long probe into the ground and set the sensor cylinder upon the soft earth. The telemetry antenna vibrated gently above it.

"Give the base a call," he said.

The base was set in a glen three miles north of Trinity Alps, a town on one of the roads that bordered the Salmon-Trinity Alps Wilderness. It was an area considerably more accessible than the one in which Ivan and Marlene Beckley operated, though a scant few miles away. A gravel road led from Trinity Alps to the camp, where there were two or three vehicles and a few tents.

A boxy van of the type used by the post office to deliver parcels and painted white bore blue letters identifying it as belonging to the National Center for Earthquake Research. Atop the van was a large, scanning telemetry antenna. Parked adjacent to the truck was another like it, but without antennae and containing the generators that powered the camp lights as well as the electronic equipment inside the telemetry truck. A half-ton pickup unadorned by markings, but clearly Army surplus, sat by the entrance from the gravel road to the camp.

A bundle of cables led from the telemetry truck to a long formica table set up in the sunlight. On the table was a radio transceiver, a mobile telephone, and a recording seismograph. The last-mentioned instrument recorded data from the various sensors planted along the Trinity Fault on a slowly moving strip of paper. Seated at the table, watching the data as it came in, was Col. Steve Austin, a handsome man in his mid-thirties with the brawny good looks of a pro quarterback.

Austin was leaning back in his metal folding chair, fingers locked together behind his head, watching a bluebird which, from a vantage point high in a Douglas fir, was watching him. The forest was silent save for the constant humming of the generator, and Austin was in an expansive mood. He liked the outdoors, especially the mountain areas when they were free of humanity. The assignment to accompany and protect the Trinity Fault expedition was one he accepted eagerly. For him, it was more vacation than work. He anticipated nothing more strenuous than keeping an eye on the electronic equipment, and perhaps, the bluebirds.

Just as the bird in the Douglas fir made up its mind that Austin was worthy of no further scrutiny and flew off, the radio crackled and came to life. The voice of Marlene Beckey was quite clear.

"Trinity Mobile to Trinity Base," she said. "Do you copy, Steve?"

Austin unclasped his hands, leaned forward and picked up the mike.

"Gotcha five by five, Marlene," he responded. "Good morning."

"Morning, Steve."

"What's your current twenty? Where are you?"

"At position nineteen on the Trinity Fault.

Ivan's planting the last sensor now."

"Any problems?"

"Nothing worth mentioning. How about at your end?"

"Not a thing. The telemetry is coming in fine. I lost telemetry from sensor five for a few minutes, but it turned out to be a short circuit on this end. A little snip of wire fell onto the circuit board and shorted out the computer input from sensor five."

"So the computer thought it wasn't getting anything," she said.

"Right," Austin said. "Like I've always maintained, a computer will never replace an old man with an abacus."

"Well," she replied, "we'll be finished soon."

"Great. Then you can watch the data come in for awhile, and I can go fishing."

"Hey...I didn't say we were coming back to base camp, only that we were finished working."

Austin frowned.

"That's unfair," he protested. "You've been out there two days. Now it's my turn."

Marlene laughed.

"Hey—when you got married did you figure you'd be spending this much time in the woods together?"

"That's *why* we got married," she replied.

"Well, behave yourselves," Austin said. "I can pick up almost anything with those new sensors you built."

"I'll relay the message to Ivan," she said. "It may cool down his ardor."

"Good move," Austin said. "I'll set up the data link for the final sensor and tie it into the printout."

Austin was distracted by a metallic, grinding sound. He looked up toward the top of the telemetry truck. The bowl-shaped antenna, designed to move back and forth in a 140-degree arc scanning the nineteen sensors planted along the Trinity Fault, had ground to a halt.

"Stand by for a minute," Austin said. "The crummy antenna's stuck again. I got to go give it a shove."

"I thought you said you weren't having problems today," Marlene said.

"The antenna was yesterday's problem," he said. "Stand by."

"Ten-four," she responded.

The radio went silent. Austin set down the mike, pushed away from the table, and hurried over to the telemetry truck. After a quick look around to assure himself of privacy, Austin bent his knees and sprang ten feet straight up to land standing atop the truck.

The shaft of the antenna, improperly lubricated by a novice mechanic who used a too-light grade of oil, had seized up again. Austin wrapped the finger of his bionic hand around the shaft just above the bearing and gave the shaft a twist. With a screech of metal, the antenna began to turn once again.

Austin stood back, admired his work and flexed his bionic fingers, which were quite capable of crushing the steel shaft instead of merely freeing it.

"An old man with an abacus," he mused. "The more I think about it, the more certain I am that I'm right."

Chapter Two

Steve Austin had good reason for his sardonic view of the accomplishments of science. He himself was one of science's highest achievements, the world's first cyborg, part man and part machine. Though very much mortal, filled with human emotions and conflicts, he had unparalled strength. He was stronger than any man had ever been, could run faster than a thoroughbred racehorse and swim as fast as a porpoise.

Actually, even before his transition from man to cyborg, Austin was exceptional. As soon as he was old enough for a student's license, he took up flying. In college he was outstanding in football, but shunned an offer to join the pros in favor of graduate school. He earned masters degrees in aerodynamics, astronautical engineering and history, and occupied what little spare time was left him with programs in wrestling, judo and aikido. Austin earned black belts in the latter two arts, then went off to Vietnam as the pilot of a helicopter gunship.

Shot down in the middle of a jungle firefight, Austin was injured enough to be sent back to the

United States. While recovering he applied for the Air Force's astronaut training program. He got into the program late. Budget cuts forced the cancellation of Apollo flights 18 and 19, which in turn forced the scientists running the Apollo program to cram three missions' worth of experiments into Apollo 17, the final manned lunar flight.

Austin was the backup pilot for Apollo 17 until two weeks prior to liftoff, when the scheduled command pilot broke his arm in a car accident. Austin was moved up to the commander's seat. With him in charge, Apollo 17 lifted off for the moon at 12:53 A.M. on December 7, 1972. It was the crowning event of Austin's life. Four days later, he became the last man to set foot on the moon. Considering NASA's budgetary problems, Austin's record will probably remain unchallenged for the duration of the twentieth century.

Like many other astronauts, Austin was deeply affected by the experience. Standing on the moon, looking back at the fragile blue-and-white ball hurtling through space several hundred thousand miles away filled him with a kind of dedication he never expected to feel. Ever since the carnage of Vietnam, Austin had been suspicious of getting involved in causes. Quite suddenly, the astronaut felt deeply involved with the Earth, and determined to do whatever was necessary to protect it and its creatures, be they humans living in cities or bluebirds sitting in Douglas firs.

Austin was on the moon three days, collecting rock and soil samples, taking pictures and setting up experiments. In all, he and his crew spent more time on the lunar surface than had any other men. When the Apollo capsule returned to Earth, Austin made the celebrity rounds expected of astronauts, appearing on television and radio talk shows and speaking before civic groups across the country. He kept it up for the better part of the year, becoming, in fact, one of NASA's greatest publicity assets. But before long the urge to fly again beckoned.

He wanted to get back into space, but astronaut assignments for Skylab and the Russo-American Apollo-Soyuz were already made. The only program left open was the Space Shuttle. Austin immediately transferred from NASA's public relations campaign to the knotty job of testing the various prototypes for the shuttle. Austin signed up to test-fly the M3F5, a nasty creation that few pilots liked. The M3F5 was a "lifting body," that is, a plane without wings that relied upon the shape of its body to get it through the atmosphere.

Pilots didn't like it, because it was neither airplane nor space vehicle. It was fired into orbit like a space vehicle, but had to coast back to a runway landing like an airplane. The design compromises necessary to the creation of such a hyrbrid made the M3F5 difficult to handle. It was unstable, a factor that wouldn't be so bad were it not for the fact that the M3F5 had to make an unpowered reentry. The pilot got one chance and one chance only at landing it. Nonetheless, Col. Steve Austin saw the vehicle as being the only way he would get back into space.

So he climbed into the cockpit of the triangular,

bullet-shaped plane while it was attached to the underwing of a B52 bomber. The bomber took off from the floor of Rogers Dry Lake in California, bearing its small companion. At the proper altitude, Austin cut the M3F5 loose, dropped a few thousand feet, then fired the main engine to push the prototype right up to the edge of space. Once again, the blue-and-white ball curved away beneath him, and for a second, he was weightless.

Then came the end of the burn and the engine shutdown. The horizon began to flatten and Austin could feel the weight of gravity pulling down on him. The heat-shield temperature rose as the M3F5 entered the atmosphere. In constant radio contact with ground control as well as the two chase planes, both Air Force jets, assigned to him, Austin brought the M3F5 into proper alignment with the Rogers approach pattern.

The experimental plane had the reputation of becoming problematical during the transition from supersonic to subsonic flight, and didn't miss the chance to give Austin a shaking around. It began to yaw, its nose waving from side to side. The ground rose with frightening speed, and the two chase planes began to bark cautions over the radio. A blowout in a damper designed to ease the yawing made the stick loose. Austin began to lose control, and so warned ground control. A frantic technician yelled at him to eject, but Austin had never lost a plane, and besides, it was too late for that. All across Rogers Dry Lake, sirens began their mournful wail. Medics and firemen poured into trucks and ambulances and burned rubber in their effort to reach the runway.

NASA personnel stood transfixed, their faces frozen with terror. What other test pilots had told them could happen was happening, and with one of the world's best-known astronauts in the cockpit. The M3F5 hit the runway with its nose too high, then slammed down, crumbling the forward landing gear. The nose dug into the surface of Rogers Dry Lake and the tail flipped up. The vehicle broke apart in a wrenching series of cartwheels, spewing smoke and fragments of metal, and for a time, drowning out even the wail of the sirens.

When Austin was pulled from the wreckage he was more dead than alive. He was flown to a nearby hospital, which NASA, with a morbid sort of concern, kept on alert during test flights. Austin was in shock four days. He lost both legs and his left arm. His left eye was also gone, torn out by a flying piece of metal that also slashed several ribs and damaged a heart valve. His jaw was crushed and most of his teeth missing. Austin's skull was seriously fractured. He was, in fact, a barely living mass of tissue. But he didn't know it. He wasn't told.

Chapter Three

Steve Austin was kept alive but unconscious, using an electrosleep process pioneered by the Russians. He was flown to the Bionics Research Laboratory, a top-secret government-funded facility in the Rocky Mountains north of Colorado Springs. There, the forces of science and government were getting together. Science had the knowledge of how to repair Austin, how to make him even better than he was. Government had the money with which to do it.

Of course, there had to be a catch. No scientific research facility can afford to spend millions of dollars on just one man. The government too was unwilling to spend a great deal of money on one man, even if that man had walked on the moon. Astronauts had died before in the line of duty, and probably would continue to do so in the future. No, if public money would go to save Steve Austin, it would have to go toward more than a straight repair job. Austin would have to be made into something special—a cyborg, an amalgam of man and machine. As the world's first bionic man, Austin would have the reasoning ability of a man plus the exceptional strength and speed of a machine. Needless to say, he would be obliged to devote his newfound powers to the purposes of American intelligence.

Ever since he read of the Bionics Research Laboratory's extraordinary successes in making human limbs, Oscar Goldman had foreseen the eventual development of a bionic man, one with superior strength; a one-man army. Thin, tight-lipped and almost entirely humorless, Goldman was a former paratrooper and ranger who had become head of the Office of Special Operations, an umbrella organization encompassing the nation's civilian and military intelligence agencies. Goldman had an extraordinary knowledge of weapons technology and an intuitive grasp of science that allowed him to envision a cyborg from having read the reports of the Bionic Research Laboratory's work. For some time, Goldman had the funds set aside for his bionic-man project. The deal he made was a simple one. The Bionics Research Laboratory would create the cyborg. The OSO would give them the sum of six million dollars with which to do it. Once created, the bionic man would work for the OSO. All that was needed to put the project into gear was the right man. The crash of the M3F5 gave them that man. The moment he heard of it, Goldman hopped a plane for Colorado.

The Bionics Research Laboratory was run under the guidance of Dr. Rudy Wells, who moonlighted as a flight surgeon for NASA and hence was also an old friend of Steve Austin. Using electrosleep,

Austin was kept unconscious for weeks. His damaged heart valve was replaced with an artificial Hufnagel valve. The crushed portions of his skull were removed and replaced with a cesium plate surrounded by spongy layers to protect both brain and skin. The plate gave Austin the capacity to endure a blow ten times harder than the one that gave him the fracture in the first place.

Austin's broken ribs were taken out and replaced by ribs made of vitallium, an exotic metal alloy much stronger than the original bone. The vitallium ribs were connected by artificial tendons, and then the entire new portion of the ribcage was joined to the breastbone with silastic, a form of silicone rubber. The vitallium ribs were laced with fine wire designed to function as a radio antenna. The antenna ran down Austin's torso just under the skin and connected to a transceiver in one of the bionic legs.

The BRL scientists fixed Austin's crushed jaw with cesium, and used ceramic to connect the metal to a full set of nylon teeth. Austin's left eye, missing as a result of the crash, was replaced at first by an artificial eyeball containing a miniature camera. The camera was capable of taking pictures that showed the image being photographed both in infrared and full-spectrum light. Austin activated the camera by pressing a button hidden under a section of the artificial skin used to repair his cheekbone. From then on, a simple blink would suffice to take a picture and advance the film. When Austin first emerged as a cyborg, the eye functioned merely as a camera, though it looked like a normal eye and moved in tune with the right eye.

Several months later, when developments in microcircuitry and neurology permitted it, the camera eye was itself replaced by a true bionic eye. A photomultiplier tube similar to that used by optical astronomers to magnify the images of deep space objects was made in a highly miniaturized form, with a zoom lens. This structure was no bigger than the old camera, and built into a similar plastic eye. The outputs from the bionic eye were patched into Austin's optic nerve. Once activated, the bionic eye allowed Austin not only to regain stereoscopic vision but also to "zoom in on" an object and magnify it by a factor of twenty. The photomultiplier tube increased the intensity of light by ten million times if Austin willed it to do so. Using the bionic eye, he would be able to see in the dark.

The bionic limbs were the most obvious examples of the BRL's artistry. To Austin's arm and leg stumps, doctors connected the bionic limbs. They double-engaged the bionic and natural bones, reinforcing the natural bones at the joining places to allow for the extra strength in the limbs. They connected actual nerves and muscles to bionic nerves and muscles, then ran the natural nerve signals through amplifiers to bring the impulses up to the level required to run the various components of the limbs. The amplifiers were fed by miniaturized nuclear generators—one in each limb. The generators, each about the size of a transistor radio, generated heat which, when fed through a thermopile, developed electricity. The electricity fed the other components of the limbs, including tiny computers into which had been programmed all the instructions necessary to guide the limbs in their task of simulating the functions of life. The controlling system was crucial. Anyone can make a strong arm. But the BRL scientists had to make one that could be tender as well. Austin had to be able to pick up an egg without crushing it.

So the technicians installed, in the fingertips and all along the skin covering the new limbs, tiny sensors that fed impulses back to servomechanisms. Servos are fancy thermostats. They function as error-measuring devices. If Austin pressed hard on something he wished to touch softly, the servo detected the error and the computer, reading the servo output, corrected the mistake. All that occurred in a tiny fraction of a second. Austin could punch through a wall, or pick up an egg or a rose petal, all without the slightest fear. To protect the complicated machinery inside the limbs, BRL technicians created a sandwich of alloys, artificial sponge and plastiskin. The plastiskin was subjected to a photochemical dye treatment so that it would match the tone of Austin's natural skin, and also tan somewhat when subjected to sunlight. Human hairs were embedded in the plastiskin. They too matched the color of Austin's own hair.

The transformation from astronaut to bionic man took better than six months, and Austin was asleep most of the time. When Rudy Wells did wake him up, it was to inform him of progress on a project that he far from fully understood. For Austin had only marginal awareness of the magnitude of what was happening to him, and no awareness that becoming the world's first bionic man would entail a rather abrupt change of career. When Wells first showed a bionic arm to him, he dismissed it as being a fancy prosthetic device. The thought of spending the rest of his days as a basket case drove him to make an attempt at suicide. A nurse prevented it, however, and Austin was sent back to sleep.

In short, Austin made at best a reluctant emotional adjustment to becoming bionic. He didn't want to be part man, part machine. He didn't want to be an "intelligence agent," and he was embarrassed by the months of trial-and-error learning that followed his "repair." Austin had to learn to walk again, even to grasp again, but this time it was while hooked up to computer banks and test equipment. He felt more like a faulty TV set undergoing bench tests than he did like a man. But most of all, Austin disliked the fact that he had not been a participant in the shaping of his own future. While he never turned down the bionics in so many words, he felt his suicide attempt spoke eloquently on the subject. However, before long Austin came to accept matters as they were. Soon he began to like his bionics. As Rudy Wells said, Austin had no foreknowledge of bionics research, so would hardly be apt to believe that such things really existed, at least not in the very short time Wells allowed him to be conscious.

A year after his accident, Steve Austin had completed both physical and emotional adjustments. He even began to get along with Oscar Goldman, though that was the hardest part of all. Goldman had made him a man once again, but a man whose destiny was controlled by others. Austin could walk, but he had to walk where Oscar Goldman told him to walk. It wasn't so much a legal obligation as it was a moral one. Austin *owed* him, and though he didn't like to be in debt, it was true and quite irreversible. Like the good Air Force officer he was, Austin went along with Goldman and became America's number-one secret weapon. After another year or so, he even got to like Oscar Goldman, and the OSO chief responded by turning a little less stiff-spined. After a few more missions, Goldman and Austin even got to be friends.

Chapter Four

The path leading from Trinity Base to the gravel road sweeping down to civilization was thick with scrub pine and meandered in such a manner that the camp was not visible from the parking area. Thus convinced he was safe from the eyes of anyone with less than a security-six clearance, Steve Austin had leaped to the top of the telemetry truck to free the stuck antenna. But as he applied bionic strength to the jammed antenna shaft, Oscar Goldman came around a turn in the path, bringing with him a man who was not cleared to level six.

The man was Tom Raintree, a scientist with the National Center for Earthquake Research, and most importantly, an American Indian born on the nearby Hoopa Valley Indian Reservation. Raintree knew the terrain surrounding Trinity Fault as well as any man, a factor equally important as his training in seismology. He was in his late twenties, of average height, but rather on the thin side. Like Austin and Goldman, he was decked out in khakis, flannel shirt and hiking boots. Unlike those two men, Raintree was cleared only to security level four. He was not among the elite group of persons with knowledge of the existence of a bionic man.

When Goldman spotted Austin atop the telemetry truck—a place inaccessible to the average man except by ladder—turning a huge telemetry antenna with one hand, Goldman froze. When he did so, coffee sloshed over the top of the container he was carrying, spilling onto his hand.

"Damn," Goldman swore.

Raintree had gotten a few paces ahead, and turned back toward Goldman. Austin was in the clear and quickly seized the opportunity to return to earth. He moved to the edge of the truck roof and dropped gently down, his feet making slight impressions in the loamy soil.

"That stuff's pretty hot," Raintree said, pointing at the container of coffee.

"You know it," Goldman said. "Here, hold the cup a minute."

He handed the container to Raintree while wiping the spilled coffee on his pants leg. As soon as he could, Goldman stole a look back into base camp. Austin was off the truck. He sighed and reached out for the container.

"Thanks," he said. Raintree blew on his fingertips to get rid of the heat.

"I've got to remember to tell old man Davis to turn down the heat on his percolator," Raintree said. "That's still at the boiling point—and after three miles of back road."

"Nice town, Trinity Oaks," Goldman said. "Small. Secluded. Quiet."

Raintree chuckled. "Like the old saying," he said, "it used to be a one-horse town, then one day the horse left."

"Come on," Goldman urged, "let's go and get you introduced to Steve."

"Fine," Raintree replied. "But tell me, why is Steve Austin working for you, anyway? Isn't he still with NASA?"

Goldman had fielded such questions many times.

"Steve and I are old friends."

"Really? How did you meet?"

"As you know, the OSO debriefs many Americans when they return from trips abroad. Because Colonel Austin travels around the world making speeches for NASA and the Space Program, he gets debriefed a lot."

The reply was the standard one used by Goldman whenever he was asked why Steve Austin was frequently seen coming and going from OSO headquarters in Washington.

"So you got to be friends," Raintree said.

"Yes. And as far as this project goes, Steve knows a lot about electronics, can fly anything ever made in case we have to take a sudden helicopter ride. And also, NASA would like to know why it was *your* scientists and not theirs who discovered the Trinity Fault. After all—"

"—The main evidence came from NASA satellite reconnaissance," Raintree said.

"Precisely."

"Well, when you got it, I guess you got it," Raintree said.

"Besides," Goldman continued, "Steve just likes the outdoors. So do I."

"This is the place," the Indian said.

Goldman inhaled deeply, dragging into his lungs the sweet fragrance of ponderosa pine. Then he sighed, and nodded in acknowledgment of the wondrousness of the area.

"You said it," he replied.

The two men walked up to Austin, who busied himself fiddling with the telemetry controls following his narrow escape from detection.

"Steve?" Goldman called.

Austin stood and turned. He was several inches taller and many pounds more massive than Raintree. The Indian was impressed. From early in his life, he learned the value of sheer size when it came to living in the woods. Austin, though only about six feet tall, weighed 240 pounds, due largely to bionic equipment. It was, in fact, the weight differential that caused so many of Austin's adjustment problems when he was learning to use the bionic limbs. For the Bionics Research Laboratory had given him not only new strength, but a new center of balance as well. It took some getting used to before Austin could run or even walk with anything resembling ease. He smiled and extended his hand toward Raintree, who grasped it.

"Steve," Goldman said, "this is Tom Raintree. He's taking over as our local contact with the Center for Earthquake Research. He grew up on the Hoopa Indian Reservation just west of here."

"One of the real native Americans, huh?" Austin

said.

Raintree smiled. "As much as anyone is native here," he said. "My ancestors may have beaten yours here by a matter of 20,000 or 25,000 years. Does that make us natives?"

"I think so."

"Anyway, I'm full-blooded and proud of it," Raintree said. "Nice to meet you, Steve. At the risk of bringing up a subject that you're probably sick of talking about, I saw you walk on the moon."

Austin smiled. "I think about it myself now and then," he said.

"It still puzzles me," Raintree said, "that I'm not sure why you two guys are here. After all, this *is* a civilian scientific project, isn't it?"

"Sure it is," Goldman said, "but one with military implications. We're here to keep an eye on things."

"Military implications? In the Trinity Fault. I—"

Raintree was interrupted by Austin, who didn't want to get involved in talking about the morality of the military.

"—If you want to know the truth about why we're here," he cut in, "I think Oscar *volunteered* us just so he could get out of his office and into the mountain air and get his fist wrapped around a can of Coors."

Tom Raintree smiled and cocked an eyebrow in Goldman's direction.

"So . . . white man speak with forked tongue, eh?" he said.

Goldman shuffled his feet and looked slightly embarrassed. "Well," he said, "maybe. Here's your coffee, Steve." He handed Austin the container and the three men sat down on folding director's chairs.

"So what's this about military implications?" Raintree said.

Goldman frowned. "You know perfectly well what I mean," he said tersely.

"You mean..."

"Geopolitics. Seismological warfare. You've heard of it. We set off an underground nuclear explosion along a major fault line in the unpopulated Aleutian Islands and *it* starts an earthquake in mainland China."

Raintree shook his head in disgust.

"Hey," Goldman said, "I'm not recommending it, just noting that it exists. The concept of seismological warfare is a realistic one—ergo, it has to be looked into. I don't create secret weapons"—Austin looked away and grimaced—"I just report on them."

"What do the new sensors have to do with starting earthquakes?" Raintree asked.

"Nothing, but they have an awful lot to do with predicting them."

"So if the Chinese try to do it to *us*," Austin said, "we'll know it ahead of time. Won't be able to *stop* it, but we'll know it."

"In this boring time of peace," Raintree said sardonically, "one must be grateful for things like that."

Chapter Five

In the clearing just up the slope from South Fork Creek, Ivan Beckey finished digging the three-foot hole for the sensor probe and was carefully lowering the metal tube into it. His wife was nearby, sitting cross-legged on the grass, frowning at her portable test equipment. The miniature computer-tester read the readings broadcast by the sensor and gave a primilary analysis of them. The analysis was nowhere nearly as sophisticated as could be had using the main computer bank back in the telemetry truck, but what it was telling Marlene was enough to wrinkle her brow.

After several minutes of frustrated checks of the equipment, she made an exasperated sort of sound and turned toward her husband.

"Are you sure you wired it up right?" she asked.

Ivan was fitting the cubical metal sensor to the top of the buried probe. Atop the box, the eighteen-inch whip antenna swung wildly back and forth with every motion of the sensor.

"What?" he asked.

"I said, did you wire it up right?" she asked

again.

"What're you, kidding? Sure I did. What's wrong?"

"I'm not sure. Let me try it one more time."

She bent over the portable tester and twisted a dial. A few seconds later, she shrugged.

"I'm getting a strange reading," she said. "It's as if there was a high-pressure volcanic vent in this area."

"Where?" Ivan asked.

"Right over there," she answered, pointing toward Battle Mountain. "That's the origin point of the readings, a little way up its west slope."

Ivan looked over at the mountain, cupping his hands over his eyes to cut out the rays from the morning sun.

"That's ridiculous," he said.

"I *know* it is. There's no current volcanic activity around here. No history of it in *this* spot at all."

"That's why our sensors are so special," her husband said. "We're gonna start *making* history with 'em."

"Even so," she said, still quite puzzled, "right now I'd forget making history and appreciate having the thing make sense."

"Well, okay," Ivan replied, "maybe our test equipment is on the fritz. Check the base readings."

"You're on," she said. She picked up the microphone and flicked on the radio.

"Trinity Mobile to Trinity Base."

The radio crackled with the characteristic snap made by a push-to-talk button being depressed.

"Trinity Base."Austin said. "Go."

"Steve," Marlene said, "have you got the data link set up yet?"

"That's a four," Austin said. "We're hooked up and ready to go."

"Did you cure your antenna problems?" she asked.

"For the moment, anyway."

"Okay," the woman replied. "We're gonna feed you some signals. Watch for anything unusual."

Ivan Beckey flicked on the transmitter section of the sensor.

"We're transmitting," Marlene said.

"Gotcha," Austin answered, watching as a read-out screen on the table in front of him came to life. Both Goldman and Raintree moved in closer, their interest piqued by Marlene's mention of the word "unusual."

Austin watched the screen for a minute, then brought the mike to his lips.

"Trinity Mobile . . . looks like you're sitting right next to a volcanic vent," he said.

"What? That can't be right," Tom Raintree said.

"Hear that?" Austin asked. "That was Tom."

"Tell him we agree. Our equipment showed the same thing. Stand by."

"Let me recalibrate the sensor," Ivan said, bending grimly to the task. Scientists, no matter how often they profess a take-it-as-it-comes attitude, don't like to see things go wrong with their brain-children. Ivan Beckey had a definite aversion to flaws appearing in the veneer of his work.

Marlene watched as her husband lifted the delicate mechanism from the ground and began unscrewing the bolts that held secure the circuit access door.

"It can't be wrong," he muttered. "We've put out enough of these sensors already, and none has gone off the bat before."

His wife didn't reply, but crawled close to him and watched as he pulled open the small metal door to reveal a gleaming and very complex circuit board underneath.

"A little piece of tinfoil could land on that board," she said, trying to be helpful, "and mess everything up."

"A little piece of tinfoil," he replied tersely, "can't invent a volcanic vent."

Marlene shrugged and resumed her cross-legged position, watching her husband as he worked, both completely unaware that a score of yards away, hidden in a thick stand of small redwoods, a very large, very strong and very dangerous creature was watching them.

Sasquatch was close to eight feet tall, slightly stooped like one of the great apes and covered with thick, brown hair. His arms spanned ten feet and could lift two men rather easily. His face was round, with the brow slanting sharply backward, and he had the thick, projecting jaw typical of various manlike primates thought to be possible ancestors of man.

Though he could stand upright, he preferred to walk or run while slightly stooped, and tended to swing his arms loosely from their joints in the manner of an ape. For several centuries Sasquatch, like the Yeti of the Himalayas, lived in legend among the human tribes that intruded upon his territory. And for the past century, he, like his presumed cousin the Yeti, had been hunted by a curious combination of scientists, adventurers and fools, all determined to know if indeed such a creature existed. Those Indians who saw or heard of him called him Sasquatch. The white man, with his unceasing talent for practicality, called him Bigfoot.

As Marlene and Ivan Beckey sat absorbed in the intricacies of their sensor's silicone chip circuits, Sasquatch pushed aside two small redwoods and stepped out into the open, a three-foot-high smattering of underbrush doing nothing at all to hold him back.

The Beckeys took no especial notice of the crackling of small bushes being stepped upon and twigs being broken. After all, in the woods there is almost always something stepping upon something; a chipmunk in search of nuts, perhaps, or maybe a field mouse seeking grains.

Sasquatch took two quiet steps in their direction when he was stopped by the noise of the radio. Austin's voice came through clearly, as if he wasn't really miles away at all. The voice gave the huge creature pause, and he cocked an ear toward the radio.

"Trinity Base to Trinity Mobile," Austin called, "any progress?"

Marlene picked up the mike without turning away from the sensor.

"We copy, Steve. We're cycling the manual override on the chip circuit."

"Find anything you don't like?" Austin asked.

"Not yet," she replied, "but if we do, you'll be the first to know."

"I'll stand by," Austin said.

He set down his mike, and was about to stand up and stretch, when there came from the transceiver the most incredible sound—a roar, deep and ugly, and a little, female cry of fright. Across the miles of woods, in the clearing just up the slope from South Fork Creek, Sasquatch had let out a bellow and charged. Ivan and Marlene Beckey had time to do no more than twist their bodies in his direction. Ivan couldn't even speak. He sat riveted to the ground while a huge hand reached out for his neck.

Back at the base camp, Austin fumbled for the mike.

"Marlene?" he asked, "I lost you ... Marlene ... what's going on?"

Sasquatch heard the broadcast and looked down at the radio. Silently, he raised a foot and stomped down on the radio, driving it quite solidly into the ground.

"Marlene?" Austin said, unaware he was transmitting to no one. "Hello ... do you copy?"

Austin cycled several switches, and tried again.

"Trinity Base to Trinity Mobile...please respond."

But there was no one to answer. Sasquatch was gone, and he had taken the Beckeys with him.

Chapter Six

With Steve Austin behind the wheel and Tom Raintree guiding, Goldman's jeep led a three-vehicle caravan up Route 3 to a dirt road that wound westward from the northern tip of Clair Engle Lake and continued up into the mountains. The dirt road drifted off into a narrow path about two miles from the Beckeys' last known position. The path was rocky, with many small gullies and the occasional fallen redwood trunk. It was impassible even by jeep, so the search party continued on foot.

Austin was frustrated. He liked the Beckeys and wanted to help them out of whatever difficulty they had gotten into. He knew he was able to get to their last known position much faster than either ordinary man or even jeep, but was unable to do so due to the presence of others. So he slogged along at the pace of a gentle jog, muttering to himself and praying for the chance to break free.

That chance never came, and as a consequence, it took close to an hour and a half for the search party to make it from the base camp to the site of the Beckeys' brush with Sasquatch. As the range closed to a hundred yards, Austin was no longer able to contain himself. He took off ahead of the others at nearly bionic speed, and leaped over a huge redwood log so effortlessly it made Goldman grit his teeth.

Austin burst into the clearing keyed up for a fight—either that or disaster. But he found nothing. The Beckeys were gone, and most of their equipment untouched. He looked around, using his bionic eye to scan the horizon in infrared looking for the thermal anomalies that would indicate the presence of such large living things as humans. No such anomaly presented itself, so Austin tried yelling. He called out the Beckeys' names several times, but received no response.

So for all his effort, Austin found himself in the annoying position of standing there, looking around in bewilderment, when the others arrived. To make it worse, he wasn't out of breath like the others. One advantage of bionic legs is that they have their own power source and don't sap the strength of the rest of the body. Thus Austin could run almost indefinitely without becoming fatigued.

Despite the absence of the Beckeys, Austin's vitality was the first thing noticed by Tom Raintree when he ran into the clearing, sweaty and out of breath. He looked at the former astronaut in awe, then turned to Goldman, who arrived just after him, followed by a half-dozen guards.

"How does he *do* that?" Raintree asked. "Did you see him jump over that log? Did you—?"

"—I did," Goldman cut in, taking time out between pants to fix Austin with an evil stare.

"How can anyone run two miles without getting tired?" Raintree asked, this time addressing the question to Austin himself.

"Hi-test," Austin snapped. "Only top quality. A buck ten a gallon. I drink it for breakfast."

"And have racing slicks on your feet, no doubt," Raintree said. He looked around the clearing. "What happened?" he asked.

"I don't know," Austin replied. "I don't see them, and I didn't get a reply when I yelled."

"You didn't see them?" Goldman asked, with a much deeper meaning than Tom Raintree could know.

"Not a trace."

Goldman turned to the Indian. "Tom," he said, "get the men organized into two search parties, and have them go over the nearby area."

Raintree nodded, and Goldman returned his attention to Austin, who was going through the Beckeys' gear.

"Doesn't look like there was any kind of a struggle," Goldman said.

Austin picked up Marlene's backpack and peered into it.

"Here's their gear," he said, "and the test equipment's still here."

Austin saw the radio, embedded four inches in the ground, with only its burnished black top visible.

"And here's the reason we lost radio contact. Look at this, would you?"

Austin and Goldman bent over the crushed radio.

"What the devil could do that? I mean, other than

you, Steve?"

"I'm not so sure I can," Austin replied. "A sledgehammer, maybe. Unfortunately, I don't see one around."

Goldman got to his feet and continued his inspection of the clearing. After a few seconds, he found the hole in which Ivan had buried his sensor probe.

"A sledgehammer isn't the only thing that's missing," he said.

"What?" Austin asked.

"The sensor—it's gone. Have a look."

Austin peered down into the hole.

"You're right. The rest of the test equipment is here, but—"

"We've got to find that sensor," Goldman interrupted.

"Yeah—not to mention our two friends. I just don't understand what could've hauled them off like this, so fast, and without them getting a chance to say something on the radio, rest its soul."

"A kidnapping?" Goldman offered.

"I doubt it."

"The sensor is gone, remember."

"Yeah, but there are a couple dozen others strewn along the fault as well as along the San Andreas Fault. If somebody wanted one of the sensors, he could do it a lot more easily than would be involved in grabbing Marlene and Ivan."

"You got a point."

It was then that they heard Tom Raintree's cry. "Steve, Oscar!" the man yelled. Both Austin and Goldman wheeled in the direction of the sound. It came from a dense thicket to the east of the clearing.

"Tom, where are you?" Austin yelled.

"Here!" the Indian yelled back.

Austin scanned the thicket in infrared and soon found the man squatting low, tracing the outline of something in the ground with the tip of his finger.

"What is it?" Goldman asked, "did you see them?"

"No," Raintree said, "but I found something else."

Austin and Goldman hacked and pushed their way to the spot where Raintree was located. As they bent over to look, Raintree pointed out a footprint left clearly in an area of soft mud. The footprint was better than eighteen inches long and six inches wide.

"What is it?" Goldman asked. "A mountain lion?"

"Not that big," Austin said. "A sizable grizzly, Tom?"

Tom Raintree was bent low over the footprint, shaking noticeably. Though a trained scientist, he had never quite forgotten the legends of his childhood, and one prominent legend was returning to upset him.

"No—no," he said uncertainly, "not a cat, not a grizzly."

"What, then?" Goldman asked.

"Only one thing in the mountains leaves a track like that—the creature of legend that roams the timberline. My people named him Sasquatch. The white men called him—"

"—Bigfoot," Austin cut in.

Chapter Seven

The three men paused for a moment to consider the enormity of what they were discussing. Then Goldman, ever the pragmatist, stood up straight and decided to disassociate himself from any theory that considered that watermelon-sized footprint to be of living origin.

"Now wait a minute," he said, "I thought that was all proven to be a hoax."

"It's not a hoax," Raintree said.

Goldman found himself on the verge of chuckling, something he didn't want to do, as Raintree obviously took the matter quite seriously.

"Tom, come on, doesn't it seem a little ridiculous to believe?"

Raintree looked up hard at Goldman. He was very serious indeed.

"It's not a hoax," he insisted. "Stories of Sasquatch go back generations among my people."

"But, Tom, aren't they mostly just superstitions?"

If it was superstition, the story of Bigfoot was one superstition that held influence even in a scientist's mind.

"Some are," he said, "but too many incidents are unexplained, eerie. When I was a boy on the reservation, I once saw a man who had disappeared for many days here in the deep woods. My grandfather was the one who found him and brought him back. There was a footprint like this one nearby. My grandfather told me that the man had seen the Sasquatch—I'll never forget how that man looked—his eyes like those of a drugged man."

Goldman allowed a respectful silence to sink in before dragging everyone back to reality.

"All right, listen," he said. "Whatever's happened to them—they've got to be found, and quickly."

Austin stood and nodded in agreement.

"I want everyone to fan out and cover the whole area," Goldman snapped. "And stay in touch in case—" he glanced at the huge footprint—"in case you find *anything*."

Tom Raintree snapped himself out of his Bigfoot-inspired reverie and hurried off to organize the search parties and give them new instructions to include a wider area. Austin and Goldman stood staring into each other's eyes for a second or two, then Austin sighed and pointed off toward Battle Mountain.

"I'm going that way," he said.

"Up the mountain?" Goldman asked. "Why?"

"Not *up* it, at least not far up it. I have a couple of reasons. First, Ivan and Marlene reported a volcanic vent in that area. Second, Bigfoot is said to prowl the timberline, and the nearest timberline is on Battle

Mountain. Third . . . I just have a feeling."

"Anything on infrared?"

"Nothing. If there was a volcanic vent, I should see it. So should the Earth Resources Satellite, for that matter. Neither of us does, so somebody is lying, be it my eye, the satellite, or the telemetry-analysis computer."

"One of them has to be telling the truth."

"That's right," Austin agreed, "and I'm willing to bet on the telemetry computer. In conjunction with the sensors, it's a million times more advanced than my eye's infrared scanner or the satellite's bigger version of the same thing."

"Okay," Goldman said, "go. But take care of yourself."

"Hey, I was out of diapers long ago."

"Nonetheless—"

"I promise," Austin said, "that I won't fall down a volcanic vent and I'll try not to let Bigfoot step on me. I'd hate to end up like that transceiver Marlene was using."

Austin jogged off in the direction of Battle Mountain. Once he was out of the sight of the other members of the search party, he accelerated to bionic speed. At top speed, he could break sixty miles per hour on a clean straightaway and do perhaps fifteen or twenty in woods of the density provided by the terrain in which he found himself.

As he progressed up the slope of Battle Mountain,

the temperature dropped, and correspondingly, the density of the vegetation began to drop. Soon he was a few thousand feet above the altitude of the Beckeys' clearing, and running easily along a long, fairly straight path that was, he thought, a deer or elk trail. The timberline, that long, stark boundary where the trees meet the snow-capped peaks, loomed before him. Austin picked out an especially tall tree that had a long-hanging branch about twenty feet from the ground. He ran up to it, braced himself and jumped up to the branch, landing on it as easily as might a squirrel.

Holding onto the branch above, Austin steadied himself and looked around. To his normal eye there was nothing. But his bionic eye picked out a scrap of cloth fifty or sixty yards away, stuck to a thorn.

Austin returned to earth and ran over to the thorn on which the piece of cloth was impaled. It was quite definitely a piece of Ivan Beckey's shirt. Austin looked at it for a moment or two, then stuck the fragment into his pocket. So he was right about that area of land. Be it volcanic vent or Indian legend, something unusual was quite definitely happening. Austin jogged further up the mountain.

As Austin ran, he was being watched, but not by Sasquatch. In a darkened room blasted out of solid rock beneath the western slope of Battle Mountain, two men and a woman were clustered before a large viewing screen. The people wore jump suits—comfortable, with a slightly ethereal look about them. The viewing screen was perfectly rectangular, with ninety-degree corners, quite a feat considering its size—about three by five feet. But that piece of electrical engineering seemed, to the persons watching it, tame when compared to Steve Austin. Many people had passed their scrutiny, but no one as unusual as Austin.

After a long period during which none of the onlookers was capable of speech—struck dumb by Austin's display of bionics—one of the men found his voice.

"Remarkable," he said, in a quietly serious tone. "Look at his speed."

"It *is* unusual," the second man agreed.

"To say the least," the woman said.

"We must definitely lure him on and find out more about him," the first man said.

The woman moved closer to the screen and stared raptly at Austin, who was running up the increasingly steep slope with speed and ease that were, in fact, nothing short of remarkable.

"Yes," she said, in a manner that indicated she felt more than purely scientific curiosity, "I think that's a marvelous idea. Lure him on, definitely."

"Okay," the first man said, "he may also have some additional information about those sensors—since he seems most anxious to find the two who were embedding it in the earth. Let's give him some bait."

"The usual?" the other man asked.

"No. Whoever that man is, he may be too much for Sasquatch. I hate to say it, but it could be true."

"Indeed," the woman said.

The first man thought for a long moment, then raised a hand in a gesture meant to indicate he had an idea.

"The male Dr. Beckey," he said. "Let's send him back. We'll keep the other one. That should get his attention."

Chapter Eight

Austin reached the timberline, above which lay the tip of the mountain, covered with sun-bleached grass, and at the very top, a smattering of snow. He scanned the upper reaches of the western slope and decided that nothing further of interest lay in that direction. So he turned north and jogged along the edge of the woods, looking for anything to indicate what had happened to the Beckeys and their earthquake sensor. A half mile along, he found it.

At first there was just the suggestion of a form in the bushes. Austin came to a halt, crouched low and scanned the area. A crackling of twigs gave Austin the exact location. He zoomed in on a spot seventy or seventy-five yards into the brush, where he saw the outline of a man stumbling rather drunkenly along. It was Ivan Beckey, making for the timberline under the mistaken impression that beyond it lay the clearing from which Sasquatch had abducted his wife and him.

"Ivan!" Austin yelled. He ran into the bushes and pushed his way to the man. Beckey was dazed, seriously disoriented, with a strange look in his eyes.

"Ivan," Austin said, holding him by both shoulders, "are you okay?"

The man shook his head in an effort to clear it.

"What...? Steve, how'd you get here?"

"I've been looking for you," Austin said. "We all have."

Beckey sat down on a log and gave Austin a quizzical look.

"Looking for us? You were just on the radio—I don't understand."

Austin was speechless. Here the man was, several miles from the clearing, missing both his wife and his seismic sensor, and acting as if nothing were wrong.

As if reading Austin's thoughts, Beckey turned around and began looking for his wife.

"Marlene? Where is she?"

"I don't know," Austin said quietly. He joined Beckey in scanning the horizon, and with the silent triggering of a nerve impulse, switched his bionic eye from full-spectrum to infrared scan. To the north, nearly lost in the distance, was a very large thermal anomaly. Austin clicked off the infrared, returned his left-eye vision to full spectrum, and zoomed in on the object. Even at 20x magnification, the object was too far away to make out. But it was a man or something like it, Austin thought, only much larger. And it was moving at extraordinary speed.

"Stay here," Austin said. He started after the thing he had seen, which was running from just the spot of woods that Ivan had stumbled out of.

"Steve," Ivan called, struggling to his feet in an

attempt to follow Austin. "Where is she? Where?"

Beckey reached out for something to grab onto, but felt only air. He slumped to the ground, unconscious. Austin hurried to him and laid him flat on the earth. When Austin once again looked for the fleeing object, it was nowhere to be found.

He sighed and bent over the unconscious Dr. Beckey. The pulse was down but strong enough, and his face was pale. He looked more than anything else like the victim of exhaustion. Austin sat on the log that previously had been Beckey's perch, and carefully rolled up his right trouser leg past the knee.

Invisible to the ordinary eye, there was hidden on the side of Austin's thigh the door leading to what was, in effect, an equipment chamber, a tool box. It was a small, rectangular compartment built into the right bionic leg, and available for a variety of uses. Austin used it to hold an oxygen tank, mask and breathing tube when on missions where he was likely to end up taking a swim. One time he stored a .38 in it, and at all times kept a very small, very powerful radio transceiver. Using that transceiver, Austin could reach OSO headquarters in Washington from anywhere in the world, simply by linking up with one of the OSO reconnaissance satellites. Furthermore, the OSO could find him by triangulation on his radio signal, as long as he was transmitting. The antenna consisted, of course, of the wires built into the vitallium ribs in Austin's chest. Austin spoke into a small microphone, and received messages via a bone-conduction device implanted close to his right ear.

Austin worked his fingers under a fold in the plastiskin and pulled the imitation skin aside. Then he pulled open the access door, pressed several buttons, and activated the transceiver. He tuned the radio to the UHF frequency used by the Trinity Fault exploration team, and pressed the button that would send a hailing signal to Goldman. In a few seconds, there was an answer. The OSO chief carried a fairly bulky transceiver built into a backpack, with a large nickel-cadmium battery and a telescoping antenna. Actually, one of the guards carried it for him, and otherwise the unit remained stored in the jeep.

"Trinity Base to Austin," Goldman responded. "That *is* you, isn't it, Steve?"

"Ten four. I'm on the west slope of Battle Mountain just below the timberline. I have Ivan. He's unconscious but alive."

"And Marlene? The sensor?"

"No go, Oscar, sorry."

"Can you get Ivan out?"

"Yeah. I don't suppose you can scare up a MedEvac helicopter, can you? It would take me awhile to carry him through a couple of miles of brush."

"Can do," Oscar said. "I have one on standby. I can have it there in twenty minutes. Will they have any trouble finding you?"

"No. I'll carry him out into the open. There's a long, vertical ravine extending from about the 3000-foot level to the 3500-foot level. We're just south of it."

"Good. I'll get right on it. What do you think

happened to Ivan and his wife?"

"No idea. I talked to him briefly, but he acted like nothing had happened. He gave me the impression I was the one who was lost."

"I can't say I haven't thought the same thing now and then. Look, I can have the chopper link into our satellite network if you like. Do you want me to arrange a triangulation fix on your position?"

"Not necessary. Just get the crummy thing up in the air and I'll throw rocks at it, if I have to. It'll find me."

"Okay, Steve."

"And by the way, Oscar, you can tell Tom Raintree that the legends of his ancestors are far from dishonorable."

"How so?"

"There's something out there, Oscar," Austin replied. "Something very big, very fast and—"

He mulled over his choice of words, and finally settled on something understated. No sense in putting unnecessary alarms over the air, at least not yet.

"—And very peculiar," he said.

Chapter Nine

It was nighttime, and Goldman's men had set up a temporary camp at the end of the dirt road leading into the Trinity Alps Wilderness from Route 3. The MedEvac chopper had dropped off Austin, Ivan Beckey, and an Air Force doctor to look after the scientist. In midair it was determined that Beckey's trouble was mainly fatigue, and that his presence in the camp to tell what had happened was far more important than his presence in a hospital bed, where the food would probably kill him anyway. The guards had enlarged the clearing and set up three Coleman lanterns to provide light. In the center of the clearing a small campfire burned quietly, sending a thin string of smoke straight up into the still mountain air.

Near the fire Ivan lay sleeping, zipped into a blue sleeping bag, his head resting on a folded jacket. Steve sat by the fire, watching as Oscar Goldman sat glued to the radio, berating a subordinate at the base camp.

"Listen," Goldman snapped in a quiet but extremely determined voice, "I understand your problems, but try to understand mine. I've got a woman missing in this area with an extremely valuable piece of hardware. Now, I need that night-vision equipment so my men can continue the search—and I need it fast."

"Yes, sir," a voice answered. "We'll have it up to you as soon as it gets to the base camp."

"See that you do . . . this is Goldman, out."

"Very impressive," Austin said.

"Thank you."

"Sounds like it's gonna be awhile getting here," Austin said.

"Yeah," Goldman said disgustedly.

Ivan stirred restlessly, and the two men eyed him for a moment.

"Look, I'm gonna head on back out there," Austin said, "toward the same area where I found Ivan. I think I saw something."

"Yeah. Right. I forgot about that. You mentioned it on the radio. What was it you saw?"

"I couldn't tell. Something. It was too far away for me to pick it up even on full magnification."

"Animal, vegetable or mineral?" Goldman asked.

"Animal, possibly humanoid. Let me put it this way. If it isn't humanoid, then one very big grizzly bear has learned how to run on its hind legs."

"How big *was* this thing?"

"Big, Oscar. Big."

"Between you and Tom, I just don't know," Goldman said. He was going to elaborate further on the subject of flights of fancy on the part of his associates, but was interrupted by the return to the fireside of Tom Raintree. The Indian was carrying a large object wrapped in a blanket. He looked at Austin and Goldman for a silent moment.

"What's that, Tom?" Goldman asked.

Raintree slowly unwrapped it. "A plaster cast," he said. "I made it from the footprint I found this morning."

He took the large, heavy white cast from the blanket and laid it, upside down, on the ground. Goldman and Austin stared in awe at the impression made by the bottom of Sasquatch's foot.

"That's a big foot," Austin said, shaking his head. "It's incredible."

"What it is, is unbelievable—and I'm using that word as a descrption, not an exclamation. Be reasonable, Tom. If there *were* a creature that size roaming this country, more people would've seen it over the years. Sooner or later, the damn thing would *have* to wander into a MacDonald's."

"Some *have* seen it," Raintree answered. "and they—" The Indian decided to keep quiet after stealing a glance at Ivan Beckey, who had stopped twisting and turning in his blue sleeping bag. His eyes were open and he was staring at the plaster cast.

Raintree was a strong man, full of moral convictions as well as scientific lack of emotion. But he was frightened by Ivan Beckey's countenance, and involuntarily backed away.

"His eyes—he's like the man my grandfather found—he has seen the Sasquatch!"

Austin looked over at Ivan. The man's body was

quivering with a strange, unspeakable emotion. His eyes were locked on the plaster cast.

In the woods near the base camp, the foot after which the plaster cast was modeled stepped lightly as it made its way toward the bright camp lights. Sasquatch stooped low, pushing aside branches and vines with his gangling arms and picking out only the most twig-free spots on which to step.

The generator truck and telemetry van were in their usual positions, and the former emitted its customary hum. The infusion of a handful more guards to replace those sent off in search of the Beckeys caused two large umbrella tents to be erected near the path leading down to the general parking area.

The work table that Austin had used to monitor the various sensors placed along the Trinity Fault was dark except for the transceiver, which emitted a low light. The rest of the test equipment served mainly as a resting spot for empty coffee containers, which were piling up with awesome rapidity. Around the perimeter of the camp walked a guard armed with a nightstick and a .38 Colt. It was but a humble imitation of security, for the camp was laid out along scientific grounds, not military ones, and was to say the least, less than impenetrable.

Sasquatch crept up to the point where darkness no longer covered him, then squatted down to wait his moment. He was just outside the circle of light cast by two large electric lamps mounted upon ten-foot stands, and behind one of the stands. When the guard, making his somewhat casual rounds, had drifted off down the path to chat with some of his fellows who were sharing a six-pack, Sasquatch crept to the nearest light stand and pushed it over. It crashed, sputtering, to the dirt.

Down in the parking area, the guard and the gentlemen sharing the beer looked up and noticed that light coming from the base camp was but half as bright as it once had been. Sasquatch rushed to the second light stand and pushed it over. The light from the base camp was gone entirely. The guard jammed his nightstick under his belt, pulled his revolver and walked cautiously up the path, followed by the others.

Sasquatch took advantage of the darkness to creep behind the generator truck. As the guards moved slowly into the camp, the huge figure bent over and grasped the bottom of the truck. With a roar and a monumental effort, he lifted the heavy van, and pushing with all the strength in both legs, toppled it over onto its right side. The generator truck bit the dust in a shower of sparks. The acrid smell of gasoline crept across the ground, and within seconds was hit by a spark and went up.

Flames covered the truck and the camp was once again bathed in light. Guards scrambled down the path and dove into the bushes. Sasquatch came tearing from behind the overturned truck, grabbed the guard with the .38, picked him up and tossed him into a thicket with the same ease that a child might toss a rag doll.

"Radio Goldman," a voice in the distance

shouted. "Send the chopper for them!"

Sasquatch, having dispatched the armed guard, tore down the two tents, and with a mighty sweep of an arm, bashed in the windshield of the telemetry truck. Then, as several guards watched in open-mouthed amazement, Sasquatch ran off toward the woods, not even slowed down by the effort required in dragging a mammoth hand along the work table, clearing off all the equipment and empty coffee containers upon it.

The camp was in utter turmoil. The truck and half the camp in which it sat was ablaze. Guards were picking themselves out of the bushes, and just when they dared venture close enough to the burning truck to aim fire extinguishers at it, the gas tank blew up, sending them diving once again into the shrubbery. Sasquatch disappeared into the woods and began making his way back to Battle Mountain. He had done his job well. He had piqued Steve Austin's interest.

Chapter Ten

It was shortly after dawn cast long shadows across the base camp that Austin, accompanied by Goldman and Raintree, strode up the winding path from the parking area to what remained of the base camp. Forest rangers had put out the fire with little difficulty, and no vegetation other than the occasional pile of dry leaves was burned. The guard who Sasquatch had tossed into the bushes was bruised and had a sprained back, both injuries that would disappear in a month.

But the generator truck was a total loss, as was much of the test equipment that previously was set up on the work table. And here and there, steam and smoke rose from either the truck or the scorched ground. Goldman was astonished.

''What in the world!'' he exclaimed upon rounding the final meander in the path and viewing the scene.

Behind the remains of the generator truck was a large patch of mud, created early the previous evening when the self-appointed camp cook dumped a ten-gallon pot of soapy water. Austin, prowling around the truck, saw the mud, and in it, another Sasquatch footprint.

"Look at this," he yelled.

Goldman was over in a second.

"What is it?"

"Look for yourself," Austin replied, bending over and tracing the outline of the print with his index finger.

"Still think Bigfoot's a hoax?" Austin asked.

Goldman studied the footprint carefully.

"I don't know what to think," he replied.

Austin stood up and gave a sharp glance at the deep woods.

"Well, I'll tell you what *I* think," he said. "Those tracks lead to Marlene Beckey."

Goldman recognized the tone of voice. It was the one Austin used when he had made up his mind and was about to embark upon another damn-the-torpedoes crusade. Goldman grabbed his arm.

"But what *else* do they lead to?" he asked.

Austin paused, realized he might be getting in over his head.

"Only one way to find out," he said.

Prying Goldman's finger from his arm, Austin headed into the woods.

"Steve!" Goldman yelled, but it was no use. The second Austin was out of sight, he ran at bionic speed. The trail left by Sasquatch was clear enough. Being hotter than its surroundings, he left a warm spot—a thermal anomaly—wherever he stepped. Using his bionic eye and its infrared capability, Austin had no difficulty following the trail.

And, using their video sensors, the three persons in front of the monitor that was so perfectly rectangular had no difficulty in tracing Austin's progress in pursuit of Bigfoot. Clustered once again about the screen, they watched carefully as Austin pursued the gigantic creature.

"He has telephoto vision, too," a male voice said.

"Yes," the woman replied, "did you see him spot that footprint from two hundred yards?"

"And there must be some sort of thermal sensor. He's running much too fast to follow the trail merely by optical means."

"Infrared?" the girl speculated.

"I think so."

"A regular jack of all trades, isn't he?" a second man said.

"What about his construction?" the first man asked. "Nyosynthetic?"

"I don't know," the girl said quizzically.

"Either way, he's worth investigating."

"I couldn't agree more," the woman in the group said slyly. "Let's test him."

"Agreed," the first man said. "Let's turn Sasquatch back on him."

The girl thought for a moment.

"We could lose one of them," she said.

The first man shrugged.

"Nothing lives forever," he replied.

Austin followed the trail as it led almost straight

back to Battle Mountain. As he neared Battle Mountain, he grew uneasy. He had been there before, had seen Sasquatch there before, and suspected that he had followed the creature into its own territory. Austin slowed his pace, and began to look about him nervously. Suddenly, the forest was indeed the forest primeval. After a moment's worth of jogging, he stopped entirely.

Nothing registered on infrared. Austin took that to mean that no large living thing was present. Actually, it meant that he had followed Sasquatch into a region thick with mosses and heat-retaining loam. The infrared picture was thoroughly confused, and quite without thinking about it, he had shut it off. So when he scanned the surroundings, he saw nothing.

But Austin did hear something. It was the distant sound of branches and underbrush being broken, as though heralding the approach of a large animal. Austin listened carefully. The sound grew louder by the second. He looked in the direction of the noise, but his vision was blocked by a large, flowered thicket. It was behind that thicket that Sasquatch lay in wait, his huge hands resting, palms down, on the earth.

Austin listened for the sound of twigs breaking to start again. At the far side of the clearing in which he stood, there began the flowered thicket. Austin quite abruptly began to take an interest in it. It quite efficiently obscured his view of a large portion of the horizon. He went to move toward it, then thought better. He moved back to the line of trees and leaned against a tall, old pine. As soon as he was esconced in that position, the breaking of twigs began again. Sasquatch was on the move. Austin pushed away from the tree and dropped to a fighting stance.

The breaking of twigs gave way to the sound of distinct, very forceful footsteps. Suddenly, the thicket burst apart, and the air was disrupted by a gigantic roar.

Austin stared transfixed at Sasquatch—from his eight-foot height to his satanic white eyes—and sucked in his breath in anticipation as the giant hurtled toward him.

Chapter Eleven

The creature stormed into the middle of the clearing, about ten feet from Austin, then stopped. Perhaps in imitation of Austin's fighting stance, he stooped over somewhat, yet let his arms dangle, apelike, until the fingertips nearly touched the ground. Austin thought that whatever the animal was, he might be of sufficiently human quality to allow an attempt at communication.

"Can—can you understand me?" Austin asked.

The fierce eyes of Sasquatch burned at Steve, but without revealing whether or not the giant understood him.

"Are you—a man?"

Sasquatch bared his teeth and snarled.

"Well," Austin said, to himself really, "it never hurts to ask."

Sasquatch began moving in a wary circle around Austin, who constantly turned to face him. The creature seemed to Austin to be unwilling to attack. Perhaps that was the anomaly Austin sought.

"Hey," he said, "how come you don't want to move right in? You were quick enough to attack the

Beckeys and our base camp. So how come you're being careful with me?"

The only answer forthcoming was another snarl and another display of teeth.

"Do you have the woman?" Austin asked. "The woman? Can you understand? That woman who was—"

Sasquatch suddenly lunged at Austin, trying to catch him by surprise and fling both arms around him for a gigantic bearhug. But Austin saw it coming and leaped to one side. Sasquatch roared past him, his mammoth arms grasping nothing more substantial than air.

Austin decided on another tack. "I know what the problem is," he said. "I don't speak your language. After all, you date back to the time of the original Spanish settlers. *Habla usted español*?"

Austin's reward was another lunge, which he also managed to duck.

"Easy—take it easy. I don't want to hurt you, and I'd like to think that the feeling is mutual. All I want is—"

Sasquatch tried a third lunge, and that time Austin wasn't quick enough. The creature got a hand on his arm and flung him half a dozen feet. Austin landed on his side, rolled and sprang to his feet. Once again the creature and he faced off against one another.

"Okay," Austin said, "if that's how it's gotta be—"

Sasquatch charged a fourth time, but Austin sidestepped and drove his bionic fist into the creature's stomach. There was no effect, other than that Austin was forced to scramble to get far enough away to ready himself for another attack.

This time, when Sasquatch took off toward Austin, Austin took off toward Sasquatch. At the last moment, Austin hurled himself into the air and hit the creature with the soles of both feet squarely in the solar plexus. Sasquatch tumbled over backward, landing in the same thicket from which he first emerged.

"Had enough?" Austin asked.

The question was answered with sickening rapidity. Sasquatch was on his feet and coming back. The creature faked left, then jumped to the right, and caught Austin with a roundhouse blow that hit him in the chest, lifted him off the ground and tossed him against a small sapling, which snapped under the man's weight. But Austin jumped immediately to his feet and faced his adversary again.

They closed, Sasquatch tried to grasp Austin's head between his hands, but Steve ducked, the hands slapped together and Austin nailed the giant with a skillful combination. A right jab to the stomach followed by a monumental bionic left to the jaw left the creature howling, his arms waving back and forth in front of him just to keep Austin away.

A short distance away, the three persons continued to monitor events in their darkened sensor display room.

"Oooo . . . very nice," a man said.

"I'd say they were fairly closely matched," another added.

"No," the girl said. "That is, I don't know."

"I'll still bet on the Sasquatch."

Out in the clearing, Austin was preparing himself for another charge, when abruptly the Sasquatch stooped, picked up a small boulder and threw it. Austin fended it off with his bionic arm.

"Hey," he exclaimed, "the use of tools in combat. Indicates advanced intelligence. You have anything to say about that?"

Sasquatch had nothing to say about that. He dove at Austin, catching him about the waist and grappling with him. Austin tried to break away, but managed only to get to his feet. The creature had him from behind in a bear hug, which is what Austin assumed the giant was always trying to achieve. As the pressure from the huge, hairy arms built up, Austin grimaced.

" 'Bout enough of that," he said, gasping, and drove an elbow backwards, catching Sasquatch hard. Again the beast bellowed and stumbled backward, its white eyes glaring furiously.

Bigfoot jumped to the edge of the clearing, took a four-inch-thick tree, and pulling it from the ground, used it as a club. He advanced on Austin, and when he was at the proper distance, swung the tree like a baseball bat. Using his bionic arm, Austin blocked it. With another roar, Sasquatch swung the tree the other way, catching Austin in his normal arm. He went down, a stinging pain spreading through his upper arm.

In the sensor display room nearby, the trio watching the combat noted the development with great interest.

"Ah," one of the men said, "only his left arm is of special construction."

"So it would seem," the woman replied.

Back in the forest clearing, Sasquatch took the tree and tossed it, roots first, at Austin. But Steve rolled away, and the tree skidded uselessly into the woods.

Both Austin and Bigfoot once again squared off against one another.

"Listen," Austin said, "I'm getting tired of this. It's time to settle it. Now, would you rather like to talk?"

In answer, Sasquatch charged again at Austin.

Swearing to himself, Austin ducked to one side. As Sasquatch charged by, Austin grabbed the beast's right arm and bent it down and behind his back. Instantly, Austin was behind Sasquatch, applying pressure upward against the arm joints. Sasquatch bellowed.

"Quit," Austin commanded. "Enough is enough."

The giant tried what Austin had tried—a backward elbow jab. It missed, but it succeeded in making Austin genuinely angry. One thing he never could take was unreasoning aggression. If a man or beast fought for a reason, that was one thing. But Austin was unable to find the reason behind Bigfoot's attacks. So he gave the creature's arm a hard, bionic push upward.

Austin expected a howl of pain, and perhaps a cry of acquiescence. Instead the most remarkable thing happened. He heard the howl, but it seemed hollow, metallic, almost mechanical. And instead of pain, the arm ripped off with the sounds of metal being snapped, fabric tearing, and electrical connections shorting out. Austin was stunned. Sasquatch stumbled away, still howling. But in Austin's hand was the creature's right arm, and from the stump came neither blood nor tendon, but wires and pulleys. It was all too familiar. From deep inside the arm, a wisp of smoke from burning electrical cables assaulted the air.

Sasquatch came at Austin with a wail instead of the roar to which Austin had become accustomed. But instead of attacking, he merely snatched back his lost arm and ran off into the woods.

Austin stared after the creature while his mind grappled with the complexity of what was going on. The legend of Sasquatch went back a quarter of a millenium at least, Austin knew. But 250 years ago, no one on this planet could have constructed anything as sophisticated as that arm. Therefore, no one on this planet had. Which meant . . . ? Austin wasn't sure of anything but the utter necessity of following Sasquatch to his lair, where he would certainly be headed after suffering the loss of an arm, even a bionic one.

Austin ran. He trailed Bigfoot perfectly, staying within visual range, and no more than two hundred yards behind. The creature was slowed significantly by the loss of the arm. Apparently, Austin thought, some sort of power loss had been occasioned by the fight. He knew that the creature had to be a robot. One might make a bionic man, but hardly a bionic ape. It wasn't logical to pour millions into building bionics for a creature that wanted no more out of life than to sit, unmolested, on the ground, pulling up roots.

Sasquatch ran in a direction that took it down the western slope of Battle Mountain. A thousand feet below the timberline the creature leaped over several fallen trees, jumped a ravine, then disappeared into another ravine. Austin reached the second ravine just in time to watch Bigfoot running along the bottom of it. The ravine, dug out of the mountainside by seasonal rains, extended a few hundred yards up and down the slope. At the top end of it was a large cave, the entrance to which was partially obscured by the root structure of a fallen redwood. Sasquatch paused briefly at the entrance to the cave and looked around for Austin, then disappeared inside.

Austin hurried to the entrance and peered inside warily.

The cave was a rocky one, without the layer of earth and compost that normally lines the bottoms of caves. It was ten feet high and about as wide. It extended straight back for about thirty feet, then stopped abruptly in a vertical wall of rock.

Austin switched on the infrared scanner. It showed nothing. He stepped inside the entrance and switched from infrared to the photomultiplier. At an amplification factor of ten million, the inside of the cave stood out brilliantly, as if illuminated by klieg lights.

The cave was empty.

Chapter Twelve

Astonished, Austin walked into the cave. Sasquatch had gone into it, there was no doubt of that. There was also no doubt that he was no longer in it. So there had to be another way out. Austin moved along the walls, knocking on them for a hollow spot. He tried the ceiling, but with no more luck. Finally, he moved back to the mouth of the cave and once again activated the infrared sensor. This time he gave it longer to work. He was not looking for a body, but a slight temperature difference that might indicate a false panel leading to another chamber. After a minute, he found it. The rear wall was about two degrees warmer than the rock surrounding it. That, Austin thought, is a thermal anomaly.

Austin walked to the section and banged his fist on it. It didn't sound hollow, but it did make a different sound from the adjoining portions of wall. Austin gave the rock a harder knock. A portion of rock chipped off. He worked two fingers into the hole left by the chipped rock and pulled, opening a foot-wide section. Inside was a smooth metal door.

Austin smiled slyly and backed away from the

door. Then he ran toward it and hurled himself into the air, hitting the door with the soles of both feet. With a wrenching scream, the metal ripped apart, the sliding door falling backward and down. When Austin raised himself on his elbow, he was lying amidst a rubble of rock and torn metal, at the entrance to what could only be described as an ice tunnel.

Walls, floor and ceiling were crystalline, and glowed with a brilliant white light. Though the floor was flat, the walls and ceiling were round, and everywhere triclinic crystals projected an inch or two. Austin climbed to his feet and stood, hands on hips, staring at the ice tunnel. It had to be artificial, he knew. There was no precedent for such a structure existing in nature, not to mention one that came with a sliding metal door camouflaged with rock.

He could have turned and gone to get help. The entrance of the cave beckoned, just over his shoulder. But Austin was caught up in the mystery of it all. He had to find out what was going on. It was a curiosity not at all unlike the one that had driven him into the Space Program better than a decade before, and had resulted in his deciding to pilot the M3F5. One success, one failure. Oh well. Austin thought, I'm one-for-one. He stepped into the ice tunnel and walked cautiously down it.

The ice tunnel seemed about fifty feet long, and to end, not in light, but in a vaguely defined darkness. Austin crept down the middle of the tunnel. Nothing happened, at least not until he reached the midpoint of the tunnel. Then, quite suddenly, the light of the tunnel began to pulse, slowly, then with increasing speed. In sync with the pulsating light there came a high-pitched, piercing tone. Austin felt dizzy. He stumbled to the right and steadied himself against the crystalline wall. There was a peculiar numbness running up and down his body. It wasn't painful, though it did frighten him.

Austin pushed away from the wall and took three stumbling steps toward the dark at the end of the tunnel. He fell to his knees, then rolled onto his back. His last vision was of three figures—two men and a woman—bending over him.

"Electrosleep," he mumbled, and closed his eyes.

"Incredible," the woman looking down at him said. "Just incredible."

"He is by far the most unique man we've seen," one of the male figures said.

"Indeed he is," she said thoughtfully.

"We must examine him very closely."

"Yes," she said, "*very* closely."

By noontime, Trinity Base was not only functioning again, but outfitted for war. Army jeeps came and went, and the meandering path from the parking area up to the work area had been made into a straight road. A new generator truck was brought in to replace the burned-out one, which was hauled away. A half-dozen infantrymen paroled the perimeter, around which had been strung a crude but effective barbed-wire fence. Trinity Base might be taken again, but it would not be taken by surprise and not without a fight. The tenfold increase in traffic coupled with the evil gleam of the AR-18 semiautomatic weapons carried by the men on patrol duty was ample testimony to the seriousness of the situation, and to the power of Oscar Goldman. There were few men who could call in a division at will, and he was among them.

Goldman, joined by Tom Raintree, a ranger from the U.S. Forest Service and an Army captain, were huddled around a corkboard on which had been placed a topographical map of the region. Goldman was pointing at Battle Mountain with a stub of a pencil.

"This is the area Colonel Austin headed into," he said. "How many men are out there searching now?"

"Ninety-four of mine," the captain said.

"We've got twenty-seven out," the ranger said.

"Good. What about air support?"

"Two Forest Service helicopters with our best men in them," the ranger told him.

"By nightfall," the captain said, "we'll have turned over every rock in the area. We'll find 'em."

"I sincerely appreciate your help, gentlemen," Goldman said. "Please keep me advised."

He set down the pencil and walked away from the map, with Tom Raintree at his side.

"Worried about Steve?" Raintree asked.

"Yeah."

"He seems pretty capable."

"That he is," Goldman replied.

"Look, Oscar, I hate to say it, but I may have

another problem for you.''

''Lovely,'' Goldman said dryly.

''It looks to be a *big* problem.''

''Okay. I'm ready for it. Shoot.''

''We've got most of the data links reconnected, and the telemetry is coming in, but—''

Raintree was trying to find a way to say it. It wasn't easy.

''What?'' Goldman asked.

''I'm not sure yet, but if everything's working properly, then we may have serious trouble brewing.''

''You *said* that,'' Goldman said impatiently. ''Now, what sort of trouble?''

''Well, are you familiar with the concept of continental drift?''

''Yes, every continent rides on a plate of rock that is moving in relation to other plates. The coast of New England once was pressed against Africa, if I'm not mistaken.''

''You're not. The plates rub against each other and cause pressure, which results in mountain formation, among other things. Now, California is bisected from north to south by a fault that marks the junction of the Pacific Plate with the North American Plate. In California that junction is what we call the San Andreas Fault.''

''Right. I'm following you.''

''The Pacific Plate is moving, in relation to the North American Plate, about a quarter of an inch a year. So, one part of California is headed north, and the other part is headed south. If the movement occurred smoothly there would be no problem."

"But it doesn't occur smoothly," Goldman said.

"Right you are. The plates get stuck now and then, build up pressure and suddenly release it in one *large* movement."

"Giving us our famous California earthquakes."

"Again right. Now, we're not really sure *why* the sticking occurs. We know how to alleviate it—pumping water under high pressure into the fault, or setting off a small underground nuclear explosion. That gets the plates moving again, but in a relatively smooth movement, not a big one. So instead of one big earthquake, we arrange for a series of minor ones that do nobody harm."

"So? What's this got to do with me?"

"I'm finishing now. The San Andreas Fault is especially stuck in the region of San Francisco. *Very* stuck, in fact. If it had been moving smoothly, a shed built on one side of the fault line in 1910 would now be thirteen feet from where it was then. But it hasn't moved at all. Thirteen feet is a lot of sticking. Imagine what would happen if it let go all at once."

"I'd rather not."

"Well, you'd better start, 'cause I think we just found out what's preventing plate movement along the San Andreas Fault in the region of San Francisco."

"Oh? What?"

"The Trinity Fault, which butts up against it. And, according to the data from the new sensors, the Trinity Fault is about to let go."

"Let go?"

"There's a dangerous pressure buildup along the Trinity Fault that is about to let go. If the Trinity lets go, computer says the San Andreas will let go."

"Christ," Goldman swore.

Chapter Thirteen

The woman's name was Shalon, and she looked strikingly beautiful even bending over the inert form of Steve Austin as he lay atop a white operating-room table. Shalon and her two principal coworkers, Apploy and Faler—the men who with her had watched the battle between Austin and Sasquatch—were gathered around the table. Exotic-looking test equipment was built into a wall that had much the same crystalline glow as did the ice tunnel.

"Are we ready for a total eunasic?" Apploy asked.

"Yes," the girl replied. "His consciousness level is stable at thirty-two."

Austin's eyes flicked sleepily open. He was semiconscious under his hosts' version of the electrosleep technique, but not at all under his own will.

"Let's first determine how much of him is actually nyosynthetic," Shalon said.

"Agreed," Apploy responded.

"I suppose you want a eunasic on his garments too," Faler said with a sigh. A eunasic was work, more work than he cared to do after such a very long time locked in their compound embedded in the Trinity Alps Wilderness.

"Correct," the girl said.

Austin was in a medical examining room. Walls, floor and ceiling were crystalline, and radiated with a muted brilliance that lent a blooming, luminescent quality to everything. Workers were haloed in the light that made their images look, to a terrestrial eye, as if seen through gauze. Under the direction of Faler, Austin was disrobed, his clothes taken away to be tested. A pair of dark-gloved hands grasped one of Austin's feet and pressed a small, flat probe bearing an antenna against it.

"Right foot and leg nyosynthetic," Shalon said, reading out figures from a console to one side of the table, "or perhaps first-generation bionic."

"Mergeron power?" Apploy asked.

"No, nuclear. Left foot and leg also. And the left arm."

"What about the eye?"

"Activate the spectranalaser," Shalon ordered.

A small beam of light shone down from a spot in the ceiling and illuminated Austin's eye.

"Definitely infrared scan," she said. "No sign of celical attachment, though."

Austin's control over his voluntary muscles was not his own. He was able to think, but not to lift a finger or, for that matter, blink. Rather, he rested in half-sleep, with the feeling that he was just about to fall completely asleep, but he never did. His hosts' electrosleep machine, plus his own curiosity, prevented that.

"Let's monitor his intramuscular caladentic response," the girl said. "Get the iron bar. Is the Opticon Scolometer on?"

An affirmative response came from a worker in the far corner of the room. Another technician placed an iron bar two inches in diameter in Austin's bionic hand. The man then got a small, black metal box and placed it against the side of Austin's arm.

"Ready," Apploy said. "Sequence begin. Measuring . . . now."

Without Austin willing it, his fist closed around the iron bar and squeezed it, tighter and tighter, until the metal began to squeeze out between his fingers like putty.

"Forty-five latts," the girl said, reading off the figures appearing on her console, "50 . . . 55 . . . 60 . . . 65 . . . 67 . . . 68.4—maximum."

"Very impressive," Apploy said.

"Now, the visual macrodynamics."

Austin lay on the table, unable to help himself, while another metal box was placed alongside his head. An eye chart bearing strange figures and shapes suddenly flicked on over his head, while on Shalon's console appeared a view of the chart as seen through Austin's bionic eye.

"Activating the zoom . . . now," Apploy said.

"Twenty to one," the girl replied, "Fairly advanced—and no celical attachment?"

"Have a look at my figures for yourself," Faler snapped angrily, "if you don't believe me."

"I believe you. He's quite remarkable. Let's do

the neuroeunasic scan now."

Two contacts were applied to Austin's temples.

"Ready," Faler said.

"Sequence begin," Shalon ordered.

There was a hum and whir of computer equipment. A section of the wall that previously looked unadorned suddenly revealed a bank of electronic equipment, some of it blinking on and off furiously. The blinking and humming continued for ten seconds, then abruptly stopped.

"Sequence ended," the girl said. "Now, I want to do a ventricular probe—drop his consciousness level below twenty."

"Dropping," Faler answered.

Austin found himself slipping into sleep. He fought it, but was unable to resist. Within seconds he was unconscious. When he awoke, several hours later, the medical examination room was nearly empty. All equipment had been removed, and he was once again dressed. Austin blinked several times, then rubbed his eyes to clear them.

The knowledge that he could move his hand cheered him, and he sat up. Ten feet away, on an operating table identical to his own, lay Sasquatch, the beast's arm already reattached. Austin grimaced when he saw Bigfoot.

"*That's* a face you don't want to see when you wake up in the morning," Austin muttered. He swung his feet up and over the table so he didn't have to look at the beast. There, leaning against the wall, looking at him, was the girl. Her skin had a luxurious, tawny color, and she wore a diamond necklace over her jump suit. Austin looked at her appreciatively.

"That's more like it," he said.

"Why, thank you, Colonel," she said brightly.

"You were here before," he said.

"Yes."

"Who are you?"

"I am Shalon."

"But who *are* you? And what is this place?"

"Be easy," she said. "No harm will come to you."

"I assumed that, when you didn't kill me right away. Is Marlene Beckey here?"

"Yes. She's well. Don't worry."

"What have you done to her?"

"The same as we did to you. We examined her."

"Okay, that was easy enough. But you still haven't told me who you are, and who that creature was that attacked me."

"We call him Sasquatch," she said with a smile, pushing away from the wall and approaching Austin, "just as did the Indians long ago. He is our helper, our protector."

"A robot?"

"Yes."

"Bionic?"

She shook her head. "Nyosynthetic," she told him. "Similar to your construction in some basic regards, but considerably more sophisticated."

"Why was he sent to destroy our base?"

"Because the sensor your people were planting detected the volcanic vent we have drilled that powers our complex here. Sasquatch bought us the time that we needed to study the sensor and create a jamming device to prevent further detection."

"And then you sent him out to stop me."

"No—to test you, and to lure you in here. Since Sasquatch proved unable to *bring* you in, it was necessary for him to lure you. You've very special, Colonel Austin. Are there others like you?"

"Of course," he said, "a whole *army* of us."

Abruptly, a red light flashed on the wall. Shalon glanced at it pointedly, and smiled at Austin.

"Now, we both know that's not true, don't we?"

"Does that thing beep when *you* tell a lie?" he asked.

"No. But then, I'm not being tested. Look, I want you to rest now. Very soon we'll—I mean *I'll* be studying you some more. Then when you've answered the questions, we'll answer yours and tell you whatever you want to know."

"Fair enough," Austin said. "But if you tell me all about you, I could tell others."

"You'll never be able to tell anyone," she said smartly.

"That's not exactly the most reassuring thing I've ever heard," Austin said. "Do you say this to everyone when it's time for lights-out?"

Shalon stepped up to Austin and entwined her fingers in his hair. "Maybe this will reassure you," she said. She leaned forward and kissed him.

As she pulled away, Austin reached for her arm, but it was gone. She was gone—vanished. He looked frantically around the room and finally found her, standing near a door leading to a similarly luminescent corridor.

"How did you do that?" he stammered. "What—what country are you from?"

"Not what *country*, Colonel Austin, what *world*."

"What world," he said dryly.

"I'll be back for you soon," she said, and left.

Chapter Fourteen

Oscar Goldman sat at the telemetry table drinking a cup of coffee, and worrying, when Tom Raintree appeared with a painful look on his face. Goldman noted it, then looked away. It wasn't too hard to spot Raintree as a bearer of bad tidings.

"Okay," Goldman said, "give it to me."

"The main computers confirm our readings. The sensors are working perfectly. The information is correct."

"Then there *is* the chance that the Trinity Fault will let go—and with it the San Andreas?"

Raintree nodded.

"The computer predicts a major earthquake along the San Andreas Fault in fifteen hours."

"Along the *whole* San Andreas? All the way down the coast to Baja California?"

"According to the computer, if the section of the San Andreas Fault that touches the Trinity Fault lets go, it just might try to make up the thirteen feet it lost over the past couple of decades. If it does that, then we've got the big one we've all been dreading. You can forget San Francisco—Los Angeles—San

Diego—and every place in between."

"A holocaust," Goldman said dully.

"The computer also came up with something else."

"What? The return of the black plague?"

"There *may* be a way to weaken or actually *prevent* that major quake."

"Like you mentioned before?"

"Yeah. The computer says that if we beat the Trinity Fault to it—trigger our own minor quake or series of them—it will take the pressure off the San Andreas. Oh, there may be a few broken windows, but no holocaust."

"Could we trigger this earlier quake by detonating an underground nuclear explosion along the Trinity Fault?"

"I think so."

Goldman jumped to his feet and tossed down the coffee cup.

"Okay," he snapped. "That I can do." He waved at an aide, who came running across the camp.

"Sir?" the aide asked.

"Get me General Davis at the Pentagon. Use my top-priority code, and put it on scrambler."

"Right," the man said, and sped off.

"Oscar—" Raintree cut in.

"We can get a portable drill and sink it down—how far?"

"A few hundred feet. Computer's working on it at the moment. But Oscar—"

"What?"

"Steve and Marlene are in that area."

Goldman swore loudly and sat back down.

"Even if they're not near the detonation site, there will be rock slides. Steve and Marlene could be killed."

Goldman waved over a forest ranger.

"Mr. Goldman?" the man asked.

"Any word on Colonel Austin or Doctor Beckey?"

"No, sir. The search teams are still reporting no sign of them."

"Oscar, there's not much time," Tom said.

"What about water? You said water under pressure could do the trick."

"No time. Do you know how long it would take to run water into here? You'd have to lay five miles of pipe."

Goldman sighed and stared out into the woods.

"Where are you, Steve?" he mumbled.

The two men were silent for several minutes, until Goldman's aide came over with a portable unit tied into an OSO communications van parked a distance away.

"The Pentagon, Mr. Goldman," the aide said. "General Davis on the line."

Goldman reluctantly took the phone, then turned once more to Raintree.

"You're sure there isn't something else we can do?"

"Computer says no. I'm afraid not. I'm sorry, Oscar."

Goldman sighed and lifted the phone to his lips.

Steve Austin lay back, semiconscious, in a contoured chair in the medical examining room, with a sensing apparatus that resembled slightly a beauty-shop hair dryer attached to his head. Across the room, Bigfoot remained on his operating table, with a similar apparatus attached to his head.

Activity in the room was back to the high level Austin experienced earlier. Technicians came and went, and the walls continued to glow with a milky brilliance. Shalon walked into the room carrying a handful of recording cassettes. She went to the computer console built into the wall and inserted one of the cassettes into a slot. She pressed three buttons in sequence, and a series of figures appeared on a large monitor. Shalon studied the figures for a long time, then broke into an involuntary grin. She removed the cassette and handed it, with the others, to an assistant.

"Take this to the Council Chamber," she said.

Shalon clapped her hands to get the attention of those in the room.

"We are finished," she said. "Remove this equipment."

In a second, the room was empty. In the same way that Shalon had appeared and disappeared for Austin's benefit earlier in the day, both technicians and equipment just vanished. All that remained were Austin and Shalon and, across the room, Sasquatch.

Austin felt the pleasant sting of wakefulness, rubbed his eyes and looked at the girl.

"This time," she said, "I positioned your chair so that you didn't have to wake up and see Sasquatch."

"Very thoughtful," Austin replied. "He's still back there, huh?"

"Until we need him—"

"—You keep him in dry dock. Yeah, I know. My boss once suggested they do that with me. Just charge my batteries when I was needed."

"I take it the suggestion was never acted upon."

"Never."

"Come," she said, "let me give you a hand. We have finished, and now would you like to take a tour of the compound?"

"Why not?"

Shalon gave him her arm and helped him up.

"I'm still a little groggy," he said.

"That's the effect of the sleep process," she explained. "It'll be gone in a minute."

"We have a similar process called electrosleep," he said.

"I know of it."

"I spent the better part of a year under electro-sleep."

"During your bionic conversion?"

"That was the time," Austin said, thinking back to his many months in the Bionics Research Laboratory.

Shalon led him to the door, which opened with a slight pinging sound as they approached it.

"Just like in the A&P," he commented.

Shalon guided Austin through the many twists and turns of the underground complex. It was a most impressive sight. If Austin had any doubts about the extraterrestrial origins of his hosts, they were removed by the marvel of the compound. While some of the walls were hewn from solid rock, others were constructed of the glowing, crystalline material.

With Shalon as his guide, Austin peeked into intersecting corridors, rooms filled with electronic equipment, rooms filled with vegetation, some of it distinctly extraterrestrial, and rooms that served as resting and recreational areas. Before long they came to the entrance to the Council Chamber, where the leaders of the community met. Shalon ushered Austin inside.

Within the Council Chamber, Austin saw a long conference table much like those used at OSO headquarters. Around the table sat six or seven men and women, including two he remembered from the medical examination room. One of them, at the head of the table, was Apploy. Apploy was an older man, with grayish white hair and a dignified look. The other man Austin recognized was Faler, a young man who just glanced at Austin, then looked away with an attitude of ennui. By way of contrast, all the others gave Austin wide grins and rapt attention.

Shalon brought him to a chair halfway down the long side of the conference table and urged him to sit, which he did. Once he was seated, she walked around the table to take her own place.

Apploy rose and waved his hand at Austin. It was an odd gesture, but one immediately recognizable as a sign of greeting.

"I am Apploy," the man said, "and I'm delighted to welcome you to our colony."

Chapter Fifteen

Austin gave the people a faint smile and leaned back in his chair to listen to what they had to say.

"I'm especially delighted to welcome you," Apploy continued, "as you are a fellow space traveler."

"You really aren't from Earth, are you?" Austin said.

"As Shalon had indicated to you, we come from deep in space."

"Is that deep in space?" Austin asked, "or deep space? There's a difference."

Apploy smiled.

"Yes, there is indeed a difference," he said. Please forgive me for being imprecise. We are from deep *in* space. We *are* from the same galaxy. Our planet is on the opposite side of the galaxy from Earth. To be precise, it is in the Sagittarius arm, approximately sixty thousand light-years from here."

"Sixty thousand," Austin said dully. "At that distance, travel would by necessity have to be super-light. All of our physicists say that it's not possible to exceed the speed of light."

"They're wrong," Shalon replied.

"The point is that we have come a great distance," Faler said, "to say the least."

"Do you come in peace?" Austin asked.

"Of course," Apploy replied, a touch of irritation in his voice. "We wish to disturb the natural progression of life here as little as possible. Our mission is to study the relatively primitive, violent society on this planet, because it closely parallels the early evolution of life on our own world."

Austin was aggravated. He decided to get in a dig of his own.

"I take it," he said sarcastically, "that your society is a bit more advanced than ours?"

"Considerably more . . . mature," Apploy said.

"That's wonderful," Austin said. "That's really cute. You know, I get so sick and tired of these smug attitudes. On Earth, it seems that whenever someone envisions visiting aliens, they are inevitably so much more suave, cool and humane than we poor fools. Just once, I'd like to see Earth visited by aliens who are loonies. You know, eccentric, really peculiar. Who every so often when walking down the street will get this undeniable urge to imitate a sea gull."

These others in the room reacted to Austin's verbal assault with a mixture of curiosity and shock.

"The way you put it, Colonel Austin," Apploy said, "it sounds like a visit from persons from another world is an everyday occurrence for you. I mean, you have been, shall we say, blasé, about us. Many persons who we bring in to study become nearly hysterical."

"Perhaps it never occurred to you that being dragged into a cave by an eight-foot hairy beast would be, for the average man, at least unsettling," Austin said.

"They have no recollection of it after they leave," Shalon said.

"Doesn't matter," Austin said. "The important thing is that you do it anyway. So what if they're hysterical? Most wild animals get a little excited when they're introduced to their cage."

"Colonel Austin..."

"Forgive me," Austin said, "I guess I just don't like zoo keepers."

Apploy leaned back in his chair, grinned and shook his head.

"You are very different, Colonel," he said, "and I mean that only in the most complimentary way."

The speech was punctuated by a loud sneeze from Faler.

"Gesundheit," Austin said. "Apparently you haven't conquered all our ailments yet."

"The major ones we *have* conquered," Shalon said brightly. "But we're still plagued by allergies."

"And Faler seems to have developed a superficial allergy to your world," Apploy said.

"In more ways than one," he said sourly.

"I knew I liked him the moment I laid eyes on him," Austin said. "Not only is he flawed, he's cranky on top of it."

"Colonel," Faler said, "I promise that before we leave I shall personally go into one of your big cities—perhaps Los Angeles—and act in a peculiar fashion."

"Thanks," Austin said, "but I have to warn you. In L.A., no one would notice."

"If you could answer my original question," Apploy said. "I would like to know how you can take us so lightly."

"Well, a couple of things. First of all, I've been through some fairly fantastic things in my life. Second, being something of an expert—as we barbarians go—on space, I have long assumed that the universe is thickly populated with intelligent species. Third, you ain't the first."

"Not the first what?" Apploy asked.

"Not the first aliens to make contact with us."

All those at the table seemed greatly surprised. They had always assumed they had cornered the market on Earth.

"There have been others?" Shalon asked.

"My experience is limited to one other. It was a year or two ago, at Cape Kennedy."

"Who were they?" Apploy asked.

"Persons from a nearby star system. From the one we call Tau Ceti."

"Oh, *them*," Faler said. "If you want loonies, what about them? First there's that peculiar radiation they emit that prevents anyone else from touching them. Then they have that dreadful tendency to walk around fixing one another with wistful glances."

Austin laughed. "Yes, I noticed a trace of that," he said.

"And they're so *serious*—"

Apploy interrupted his associate. "Was your experience with the Cetians connected with that episode where you test-flew the Space Shuttle on a rescue mission?"

"That was it. We snuck the one surviving Cetian from a party of four into the shuttle and rendezvoused with her mother ship. The others were killed off by that radiation. You know, it's rather like the situation with a bumblebee. If the bee stings another bug, he dies too. If a Cetian touches an alien, both die. I was helpful partially because of this—"

Austin held up his bionic arm.

"—I was immune to that particular problem."

"Oh, yes," Apploy said, "your bionics. We're especially intrigued by your bionic construction."

"I was wondering why I was so"—he stole a sly glance at Shalon—"intriguing."

"Shalon has more questions for you," Apploy said. "Her specialty is nyosynthenics—highly sophisticated bionic construction. It was she who built Sasquatch."

Austin fixed her with a lascivious glance.

"I can see that she's a very talented lady," he said.

Chapter Sixteen

"How long have you been here?" Austin asked.

"Two years," Apploy answered. "And in that time we've had Sasquatch bring us many people to study. We have scanned their bodies, freely conversed with them, as we are now doing with you, and then returned them, unharmed, to the outside."

"And Marlene and Iván Beckey?"

"The geologist couple? Yes, they were here."

"And she is being returned outside even now," Shalon said.

"But when I found Ivan he had no memory of you—of this place."

"That is correct. Doctor Beckey and his wife, like *all* those we bring here, have their memory of Sasquatch and our colony wiped clean."

"And you'll do the same with me?" Austin asked.

"When we're finished with you," Apploy said, "yes."

"But wait," Austin said, "wait a minute. You said you've only been here two years. The legends of Sasquatch go back among the Indians for *hundreds* of years.''

Apploy and Shalon exchanged a smile.

''This is true,'' he said, ''but let me show you something.''

He produced a small object, about the size and configuration of a pocket computer.

''This is the most marvelous device that our science has yet created,'' Apploy said. ''It is a byproduct of the research that went into our spacecraft propulsion systems—''

''—The ones that go faster than light.''

''Many times faster, yes. This is a Time Line Converter—a TLC. It allows us to speed up our own individual progression through time, relative to our surroundings.''

Austin's brow developed sufficient furrows to prevent erosion of an entire Iowan cornfield. He was trying very hard to fathom it.

''So you could make a whole day pass in one minute?'' he asked.

''In one second,'' Apploy said with a smile. ''If we want. We *did* arrive 250 years ago, but as a group we've moved forward quickly from time to time, so to speak, so that while 250 years passed on Earth, only two years have passed for us.''

Austin looked around at them and couldn't help but chuckle. It was all so incredible, yet so real, his mind was totally boggled.

''It still feels like 250 years to me,'' Faler said, ''250 years of allergies.''

Apploy gave Faler a dirty look, then resumed his lecture.

''The TLC has other applications, also—''

''—Such as providing the mild amusement of being able to move from place to place—'' Faler said, touching his TLC and disappearing, ''—seemingly in the blink of an eye.'' He reappeared by the door, and his voice changed from mild amusement to intense boredom.

''Isn't it fascinating?'' he said sardonically. ''Now you see him''—

He touched his TLC and vanished again.

—''Now you don't.'' Faler reappeared behind Austin's chair, with his hand resting on Austin's shoulder.

Apploy let loose an indulgent sigh.

''Please be seated, Faler,'' he said.

The young man's temper flared.

''Listen, Apploy, just because you're the—''

''*Sit down*,'' the older man said firmly, his voice an implied threat. The two men glared at each other for a moment. Then Faler grudgingly lowered his eyes and touched the TLC a third time. He reappeared a split second later in his chair, drumming his fingers on the tabletop and very much giving the impression of being the bad boy of the outfit.

''As you can imagine, Colonel Austin,'' Apploy said, ''the hardest part of our five-year mission is dealing with the small personality conflicts that arise.''

''Yes,'' Austin said, ''it's the same way among my people. It's—''

Austin chuckled.

''Something is funny?'' Shalon asked.

"I was going to say 'it's only human.' "

Austin and Apploy exchanged ironic smiles, while Faler chose to sit glumly. Steve broke the silence after a few seconds.

"Tell me," he said, "how long did it take you to get here?"

"From our world?" Apploy said. "Approximately three of your months."

"Three months!" Austin exclaimed, "to go sixty thousand light-years. The fastest of our spacecraft would take millions of year. How fast were you traveling?"

"Superlight speed cannot be expressed in sublight terms," he said. "There are no language equivalents. I could tell you, but it would mean nothing. Don't worry. Your people will discover it in about two thousand years."

"Wonderful," Austin said. "Now if I can just get a hold of one of those TLC—maybe even get myself turned into a robot like Sasquatch, I'll be around to witness the development."

Several persons laughed.

"On the subject of Sasquatch," Austin said, "I'm really sorry I broke him. It was nothing personal. I tried to talk to him, in English and Spanish, but he kept coming after me. When you get the arm fixed, send me the bill. I'll put a check in the mail. Maybe I can take it off my income taxes."

"Don't worry about Sasquatch," Shalon replied. "He is already fixed. If we need him," she said, "he will be ready."

Back at the base camp, Oscar Goldman ran to intercept a jeep as it pulled into the camp with horn blaring. Inside the jeep were several members of the search team, including the ranger who had been reporting to Goldman on progress or the lack of it, plus Marlene Beckey. She was still woozy and shaken, but essentially unhurt.

"Marlene!" Goldman exclaimed.

She looked at him with a dull, uncomprehending expressions. It was almost as if she didn't remember him.

"Marlene—it's Oscar."

Still there was no response, so Goldman turned to the ranger.

"Where was she found?" he asked.

"In the vicinity of Battle Mountain—west slope—she had the missing sensor with her."

The ranger held up a backpack containing the device.

"It's in here and, as far as I can tell from your description of it, intact."

"Good," Goldman said. "Marlene, where have you been?" He touched her arm gently and used the most soothing tone of voice he was capable of mustering. The girl looked at him with big, frightened eyes.

"What?" she stammered, "I don't know. We were planting the sensor and then—"

"Yes? Try to remember."

Marlene strained to remember.

"We were planting the sensor, and then . . . I don't

know . . . I . . . where's Ivan?"

"He's safe, Marlene," Goldman said. "They'll take you to him. But what about Steve? Did you see Steve?"

"Steve? He was with you—talking on the radio, as we were planting the sensor. That's all I can . . ."

Her voice trailed off into a series of mumbles.

"Okay," Goldman said, suppressing his frustration only with the greatest difficulty, "you take it easy. The rangers will take you to your husband."

"I'm so confused," she said.

Goldman waved the jeep off, and it started down the path toward the road out. Soon Marlene would be reunited with Ivan. For them, the adventure had ended. For Oscar Goldman, Tom Raintree, and most of all, for Steve Austin, it had barely begun.

Chapter Seventeen

As soon as Marlene Beckey was safely on her way to join her husband, Tom Raintree accosted Oscar Goldman at nearly the northern perimeter of Trinity Base.

"The nuclear device has arrived," Raintree said. "It's a tiny one-megaton, but even that should shake things up a bit."

"What about the detonation site?" Goldman asked.

"It's on the fault line just two miles to the northwest of Battle Mountain. We've got a high-intensity laser drill going full tilt. I would say that we'll have the bomb in position in about three hours. Then we can detonate immediately."

"And trigger a quake through this region that could trap or even kill Steve."

"There's no choice, Oscar," the Indian insisted. "You've seen the computer printout."

"I know, Tom, but listen! Isn't it *possible* that the prediction of that major earthquake along the San Andreas Fault could be wrong?"

"Of course they *could* be wrong," Tom Raintree

said, "but according to everything I've ever learned, the chances are pretty slim. And we'll have a test pretty soon."

"Test?" Goldman asked. "What kind of test?"

"The sensors are indicating a minor tremor along several of the tributary faults—including the Trinity Fault, in—"

He checked his watch.

"—in seventeen minutes."

"If that minor tremor *does* occur?"

"Then the prediction of the major quake all down the California coast will be verified as an *absolute certainty*."

Goldman and Raintree exchanged tense glances.

"We'll know for sure in seventeen minutes," Tom Raintree said.

Steve and Shalon strolled down a corridor in the underground compound. She had her arm cheerfully laced through his, and seemed thoroughly enthralled with his presence.

"How much longer will you be here?" he asked.

"Our ship will not return for three more years."

"Ship?" Austin asked, "I haven't seen a ship."

"Of course not, it's not here. It will come to get us. At superlight speed, nothing is all that far away from anything else, unless you want to travel intergalactically."

"Not me," Austin said, "at least not this year."

She smiled, and squeezed his arm.

"What makes a woman attractive in your world?"

she asked.

"You've been the ones who have been studying *us*," he said.

But she was persistent.

"Come on," she said, "tell me."

"Well, it depends on who you talk to—for me a woman needs intelligence, a sense of humor—"

"—And physical, shall we say, attributes?"

"Well, every little bit helps. Why? What sort of man would *you* consider attractive?"

"A man like you," she said with a smile.

Austin looked at her, a bit uncomfortably.

"You know, Doctor," he said, "when we first met, your 'bedside manner' surprised me a little."

Shalon was slightly embarrassed.

"Do you treat all of your patients that way?" he asked.

She laughed with her own embarrassment.

"Of course not, but I have been cooped up here for two years with a group of very stuffy scientists. Then you came along like a breath of fresh air—not only intelligent and witty, but also bionic, my specialty. Well, like you said, every little bit helps."

They smiled at each other for an extended moment, then she squeezed his arm meaningfully.

"There's an operation I'd like you to help me with," she said.

"Sounds good," Austin said. "What sort of operation?"

"One I think you'll enjoy," she said slyly.

At Trinity Base, Goldman, Raintree and several other men gathered about the work table, awaiting the return of telemetry information on Raintree's projected small tremor.

"Fifteen seconds," the Indian said, nervously checking his watch and toying with a container of coffee.

Goldman had a telephone pinned between his cheek and his shoulder.

"That's right, General," he said into the telephone. "If this small tremor occurs as predicted, then the major earthquake along the coast will follow in seven hours and forty minutes."

"Eight seconds," Tom Raintree announced.

"Stand by," Oscar said into the phone.

"Six seconds," Tom announced, reading from the dial of his watch. "Five . . . four . . . three . . . two . . . one . . ."

There was a pause, a long pause. Nothing at all happened. Goldman and Raintree exchanged quizzical glances. The latter quickly punched an instruction into the computer, and got an instant readout.

"That should have been it," he said. "The small tremor should have hit us. The computer confirms it."

"The sensors must be wrong, then!"

"Maybe so."

"No tremor now," Goldman said, "no major earthquake later."

"Could be," Raintree said, acquiescing willingly. He didn't want to see Austin injured any more than Goldman did.

"Thank God," Goldman swore. "I'll sign the release papers and get that nuclear warhead back to the arsenal."

The men around him likewise breathed sighs of relief and began to chat informally among themselves. Tom Raintree bent over the release papers, studying them, while Goldman tried to wrap it up with the Pentagon.

"General," he said into the phone, "good news. The expected tremor did *not*—repeat *not*—arrive. It looks like everything will be—"

Oscar stopped talking. A low rumble filled the hills, scaring the birds into flight as it built in intensity. Sitting atop the radio, Tom Raintree's coffee cup began to vibrate, spilling brown liquid onto the equipment. The tremor had come. The coffee cup vibrated toward the edge of the radio, then fell off, dropping its contents onto the release papers Goldman was about to sign that would send the bomb back to its arsenal.

After two or three minutes the tremor abated. Coffee cups were retrieved from where they landed on the ground, and chocks were adjusted under truck wheels to prevent rolling.

Goldman stood silently, the phone link to the Pentagon still in his hand. On the other end of the line, General Davis was bellowing into the phone, trying to find out what happened.

"It's all Austin's fault," he mumbled. "All year long all I hear is 'let's take off for a week, Oscar. Let's get out in the woods and breathe some fresh air, Oscar. 'Hell, if I had this week to do over—''

''You'd do it differently?'' Tom Raintree inquired.

''I wouldn't do it at all.''

Chapter Eighteen

Within the underground complex, Austin and his extraterrestrial hosts were also feeling the effects of the tremor. The low, rumbling noise drowned out the persistent whine of the crystalline walls and ceiling. Equipment began to rattle, and an occasional piece could be heard crashing to the floor.

Several people were in the main corridor, grasping the walls for support. One lady lost her grip and tumbled to the floor. Dust was all over like a thin, gray blanket. Austin looked at the gray blanket, and at the fallen woman. Then he looked at the portion of ceiling above her, zooming in close with his bionic eye. He saw a small crack turn into a big crack, then start to widen ominously, threatening to spill its contents onto whomever was so unfortunate as to be below.

Austin bolted with bionic speed up the corridor. A large stone section slipped downward an inch. There was little question but that it would fall, and right on top of the dazed woman. Austin reached over his head with his bionic arm and pressed hard against the falling stone. Shalon watched Austin fearfully as the tremor continued. Two minutes later, it started to abate. The tremor was passing, but Austin still held up the ceiling in that portion of the main corridor.

As the earth stopped rumbling, some of his hosts regained their senses and pulled the woman to safety.

"Quick," Shalon yelled, "get an emergency support column."

A technician scurried off, and less than thirty seconds later, reappeared carrying a long support column. As Austin pushed up on the stone, Shalon and the technician inserted the support column between the floor and the falling stone.

"I'm gonna let it down now," Austin said.

"Right . . . easy," the technician replied.

Austin lowered the stone until it rested easily on the steel column.

"Good," the technician said. "Good. That's got it."

Shalon hurried over to Austin and wrapped her arms around him.

"Are you all right?" she asked.

"Sure."

"So that's an earthquake."

"Aw, just a little tremor," Austin mused. "Nothing at all to worry about."

At Trinity Base, Tom and Oscar were mulling over the tardiness of the tremor, while General Davis continued to hold the line.

"I found the computer error," Raintree said. "One figure had been entered wrongly. The tremor *did* come exactly when the sensors predicted."

"Then—the major earthquake predicted for the California coast?"

"Is a *certainty*—seven hours and thirty-six minutes from now."

"All right," Goldman said with a tense sigh. "We've got no choice. We must proceed with the nuclear detonation. Keep them moving, Tom."

"Right," the Indian said. He turned to leave, then turned back.

"Any word about Colonel Austin, Mr. Oscar?" he asked.

Goldman looked at the man and simply shook his head slowly. Raintree looked back, searching for words. He found none, so just gave Goldman a forced smile and a pat on the shoulder.

Steve Austin and the girl stood in the medical examining room, staring down at Sasquatch as the beast lay upon his operating table.

"Boy," Austin mused, "that's a face only a mother could love."

"He's very sweet," Shalon said, "once you get to know him."

"He *is* turned off, isn't he? I would hate to have an impromptu replay of our last encounter."

"Sasquatch," she said, "is quite definitely turned off."

Various electronic tones filled the room as Shalon and Steve worked to repair the gigantic creature. She was doing most of the work, with Austin functioning as avid student and chief nurse.

"How come you're doing the shoulder over?" he asked. "You told me before it was hooked up again and working fine."

"That was before. In the meantime, I got an idea that could give him additional strength—just in case he ever has to take on your 'army' of bionic men."

"Have you made others like him?" Austin asked.

"No. He's my baby. The very first one."

Shalon requested a scalpel, and Austin handed one to her.

"Why don't we have to wear surgical outfits?" he asked. "In the manufacture of even our most simple satellites, all work is done under sterile conditions."

"The air in our medical chambers is hyper-sterilized," Shalon replied. "No bacterial agent—or speck of dust, for that matter—can survive. And even if it did, neotraxin 3 would take care of it."

"Neo—what?" he asked.

"Neotraxin 3," she said proudly. "I'll show you a vial sometime. It's an electrolytic neuroprobesis that works with the DNA in our bodies to check the spread of disease."

"Which disease?"

"Used in concert with various other compounds," she answered, "it takes care of *all* diseases. Neotraxin's the basis for all our 'wonder drugs.' "

She bent over the inert creature and patted him on the chest.

"There you go, big fella," she said, "You'll be better in no time."

"You're really attached to him, aren't you?"

''There's very little else down here to be attached to.''

Steve and the girl exchanged friendly glances, then she returned to her work, searching through an instrument tray for a utensil. She was looking for a specific instrument, but couldn't locate it. The closest she came was a needle-nosed pliers.

''I can't find the right instrument,'' she complained, holding up the pliers. ''Like this, only curved.''

Austin took the pliers from her.

''Here,'' he said, ''see if this'll work.'' He bent the nose of the pliers into a gentle curve, then handed the instrument back to the girl. She smiled, took the newly created tool and made a final adjustment.

When finished, she dropped the pliers into her instrument tray and pushed it into its hiding place under the table.

''Okay,'' she said, ''his arm is reconnected and strengthened. Even *you* couldn't pull it off now.''

''I've got no desire to try,'' Austin said quickly.

''The final step,'' she continued, ''is to reinsert the mergeron power cell—on the block there.''

She pointed out a small, square black box with an array of contact strips located around its perimeter.

''This?'' Austin asked. ''This is the power cell that runs this ridiculous contraption? It's very small. What's mergeron?''

''An antimatter power source,'' she told him. ''Your people will discover it in a century or so.''

While Austin mulled over the possibilities inherent in an antimatter power source, the girl returned her attention to Sasquatch.

"That neotraxin serum of yours sounds even more important than mergeron," he offered. "I was thinking of all the lives it could save among my people. I don't suppose there's any chance you might—"

Shalon smiled at him, paused thoughtfully, and then flashed a coquettish grin.

"Well, of course, we've never allowed anyone before to leave with any of our secrets," she said, "but perhaps if you considered remaining here for a while—letting us study you more closely—strictly for our research, of course."

Austin returned her coquettish smile.

"Of course," he said, "strictly for research."

It was a double game that they both were playing, and both were bright enough to recognize it.

"Stay for a while, huh?" Austin mused. "Well, I might be able to do that—but I'd sure like to get a message out to let my people know I'm all right."

"Not possible," the girl said hastily. "Apploy won't allow it."

"Not even ten seconds' worth of Morse code?"

"Not even a smoke signal," she said.

"But—"

Shalon ignored his protests, leaned to him and kissed him a second time.

"Just for science?" he asked.

"Just for science," she replied.

Immediately, both of them broke out into laughter. When that ended, they embraced. Austin held her for a long moment, until they were interrupted by the sound of a message tone.

Reluctantly, Shalon disengaged herself from Austin's arms and pressed a button on her test console. Apploy's image appeared on the visual communicator.

"Shalon," he said, "come at once."

"I will," she replied.

The screen went blank and Shalon again gazed at Austin—a gaze that carried messages of thanks, and other emotions.

"Please wait here," she said, and hurried out of the room.

Chapter Nineteen

As soon as the girl was gone, Austin hurried to the communicator and pressed a button. A view of a corridor popped onto the small monitor. He tried another, and was rewarded with a view of the recreation room. Finally, through the process of trial and error, Austin found the buttons that displayed the scenery taken in by the outdoor sensors. In particular, he found the sensor that was trained on Trinity Base.

He got a picture of the working area, with Oscar and Tom seated in front of the telemetry readouts, the exact seat Austin occupied before the adventure with Bigfoot started. After fiddling with a few more dials, Austin managed to get audio as well as video from the screen. While Austin was making adjustments in the communicator, the Army captain who was helping out joined Goldman and Raintree. Austin grinned as the sound cracked on.

"Have the grid coordinates come in yet?" Goldman asked.

"Just got them," Tom said.

Austin decided to see if the gadget worked both

ways.

"Oscar," he said, "Tom . . . can you hear me?"

But they couldn't hear him. They continued talking, oblivious to Austin's long-range observation.

"The nuclear warhead is in place," Tom said.

"Nuclear warhead!" Austin exclaimed. "Tom . . . can you hear me? Oscar?"

"Exactly what are we expecting?" the Army captain asked.

"Run down the timetable for the captain, Tom," Goldman said.

"Okay . . . the detonation will occur at Station 19 at 1608 hours. This will trigger a quake along the Trinity Fault which should peak at 7.9 on the Richter Scale."

"Seven point nine?" Austin said.

As if in answer, Tom Raintree explined.

"That's a pretty big quake," he said, "but remember that it's located in an unpopulated area. The Trinity quake should relieve the pressure on the San Andreas Fault—hopefully preventing a major earthquake on the California coast. It's now due in five hours."

"What?" Austin yelled, quite shocked.

The noise roused more than Austin's ire. It woke up Sasquatch, who had been disconnected from the sleeping process and allowed to come around in his own good time. He opened an eye and stared at Austin, who had his back to the creature.

"All right," the Army captain said. "The area surrounding the fault line in the region of the west slope of Battle Mountain has been cleared. When your man-made quake tears through these mountains, Mr. Goldman, there should be no one in there—except, of course, Colonel Austin."

Goldman and Raintree exchanged concerned glances. Then Tom checked a digital counter and flicked the switch on a PA system, amplifying his voice so that it might be heard by the entire camp.

"Countdown to nuclear detonation is at . . . mark . . . twelve minutes."

Bigfoot's head was clearing, and he raised himself on one elbow to get a better look at what Austin was doing. Unaware he was being watched, Austin tried the UHF transceiver built into his right leg, only to discover that his hosts had disconnected it. The wires leading to the power source were cut, and Austin had no time to splice them. He rolled his pants leg back down and hurried from the room.

With some difficulty, and the waste of three minutes, Austin found the Council Chamber and burst inside. Within its confines, Apploy, Faler and some the others were talking quietly. Shalon was conspicuously absent.

"Apploy," Austin said, "a major earthquake's been predicted along the coast, and my people are going to trigger an earlier quake *through these mountains* to try and stop it."

"Yes," the older man said, "we know."

"What? You *know* about it?"

"That's right."

"But your complex here is in a lot of danger."

"No," Apploy said, "no danger. The man-made earthquake will simply not be allowed to happen."

"What do you mean?" Austin asked.

"Shalon has been dispatched to the nuclear detonation site. She will disable the detonator and prevent the explosion."

"But you don't seem to understand," Austin protested. "If the pressure isn't releaved by causing that quake here in the mountains, then a really *bad* quake's gonna strike all along the California coast."

"We understand," Apploy said.

"But that's one of the most densely populated areas in the country. Even *with* adequate warning, a lot of people could be killed. Thousands . . . millions."

"I am sorry. There is nothing I can do."

"Of course there is," Austin yelled. "Stop Shalon. And evacuate your complex here."

"That," Apploy said, "is regrettably impossible."

"Regrettably? What do you mean, regret? I get the impression that all you *do* is regret. You drive people half nuts by having Sasquatch haul them in here. You regret it, and think that by erasing their memories you have erased the fact that you caused them to experience terror. How could you tell me what a *mature* society you have—compared to us primitives—and now stand by and allow the deaths of so many innocent people?"

"Sacrifices have been made in the past. It is the price that must be paid for scientific advancement. That's all that I can be concerned about."

Austin was fuming. "The right of my people to live takes precedence over the right of your people to be zoo keepers,'' he yelled.

Austin wheeled around and made for the door.

''Let me warn you,'' Apploy said, ''that any attempt to escape will be futile.''

''We'll see about that,'' Austin said as he stormed from the room.

Chapter Twenty

The second Austin was out in the main corridor, he wheeled and ran as fast as was possible within the confines of the underground complex. Though the corridors were many, Austin had a good idea of where the exit lay and a certain amount of confidence about his chances of making it. In the time he was there, not one weapon was in evidence, and he felt it likely that his hosts considered the use of weapons to be vulgar. They thought themselves so far above any use of force, they wouldn't even allow their dirty work to be done by a creature resembling one of them. Instead, they built a mechanical henchman based upon some lower order of primates and consigned to him all the nasty business. The more Austin thought about it, the madder he got and, fortunately, the faster he ran.

After a hundred feet or so, the main corridor intersected with a narrower, darker hallway hewn out of rock. Far away, at the end of it, he could see the luminosity of the ice tunnel. Austin started down the hall. Before he had taken three strides, he felt a strange rush of air, as if something had run by him at incredible speed. Then, Apploy, Faler and several other men appeared from nowhere, blocking his path. They had used their Time Line Converters to get in front of him. Austin ground to a halt thirty feet from them.

"I beg you, Colonel Austin," Apploy said, holding up his palm in the gesture of 'stop,' "for the sake of yourself and my people—don't try to escape."

"Listen," Austin snarled, "I've gotten sick and tired of playing Noble Savage for the amusement of you and your crew. Now, are you gonna stand aside or do we have to do this the hard way?"

"Colonel—"

"All right," Austin said, matter-of-factly, "you came here to study violence."

Austin dropped low into the position of a linebacker blitzing a weak line, and charged into the group of men at bionic speed. He plowed through them, whipping his elbows apart to send Apploy crashing into one wall, Faler the other.

"Now the poor bum's gonna have a backache on top of his hay fever," Austin mused as he continued on down the hall.

A whining electronic alarm rang out through the compound. As if on cue, two men ran out from a side corridor and into the rock-hewn one down which Austin loped. They squared off to face him, but as they obviously had never tackled anything more dangerous than an undercooked meal, weren't too frightening. Austin stopped near them.

"You don't really want to get involved in this, do you?" he asked.

“No, but we have our duty,” one of the men said.

“Okay, which one of you wants it first?” Austin asked, making an elaborate show of rolling up his sleeves.

“Uh—maybe we can think about duty tomorrow,” the other man said.

“Very wise,” Austin said, “very wise. Now, if you will excuse me . . .”

He walked by the two men, who flattened themselves against the walls to avoid being touched by him. Austin was unable to suppress a giggle. He had found their Achilles’ heel. They were so convinced that Earthmen were savages, they were prepared to accept the slightest hint of threat as being a declaration of impending slaughter. While entertaining the thought of getting Apploy into a poker game, Austin continued down the hall.

Fifty feet from the ice tunnel, he again halted. Using his bionic eye, Austin searched the rocky ceiling, looking for a weak spot, preferably one with a good hand-hold. After a few seconds, he found it. Austin reached up with his bionic arm and tugged down on that section of ceiling. A trickle of dust fell on his shoulder. He tugged harder. There was a low, groaning sound from the rocks above him. Finally, Austin pulled down with all his strength. The moaning increased, but no rocks came with it. Frustrated, Austin cocked his first and drove it into the ceiling. The moaning changed into a roar and the rocks came down, forcing Austin to roll-dive out of the way.

When he regained his footing, Austin saw that the tunnel was blocked three-quarters of the way to the ceiling. He wiped his hands on his pants and turned toward the ice tunnel. Secure in the knowledge that the compound's technicians would take a good while to dig through the rock pile, Austin walked slowly to the edge of the ice tunnel.

The glimmering passage would look beautiful at any other time. But the ice tunnel, the compound's introductory course in what they called "the sleeping process," had begun to pulse, both in light and sound. It was emitting the waves that matched the wave forms of a man's brain and lulled him, rather abruptly, to unconsciousness. The tunnel was fifty feet long. Austin recalled that when he first entered the tunnel, sleep didn't overtake him until he was halfway down it. Maybe if he was fast enough...

But the thought suddenly disappeared. For at the end of the ice tunnel, framed against the repaired metallic door, stood Sasquatch, in full strength and bellowing at the sight of Austin. Austin placed his hands on his hips and sighed.

"Not again," he mumbled.

Back down the rocky hallway, a group of compound technicians were frantically working to clear the debris Austin had left there. Well, Austin thought, I can't handle Bigfoot and the ice tunnel both at the same time, so I'll have to get him out of there. Funny, Austin thought, now it's *me* who's trying to lure *him* into the compound.

"Hey," Austin yelled, "what would you like removed this time? A foot?"

Bigfoot bellowed. Perhaps he understood English, perhaps not. Probably he was programmed to respond to a threat sound with a louder threat of his own. Indeed, the creature had followed Austin's taunt with a roar. Well, Austin thought, let's try it again.

He remembered that when Sasquatch threatened, he waved his arms back and forth over his head. Many animals try to give the impression of increased size while threatening an opponent. So Austin stuck his hands over his head, waved them around and gave a rough imitation of Bigfoot's roar.

The creature turned livid with rage. It repeated its threat, but stayed at the far end of the ice tunnel.

"I don't care if he doesn't come at me," Austin grumbled, "I'm not gonna do *that* again. My dignity is worth *something*." He decided to try a different tack. He sat down.

Sasquatch stared at Austin quizzically. He was programmed for fear or attack, but not for an adversary that sits down and ignores him. After a minute of staring each other down, Sasquatch began to move cautiously toward Austin. When the beast was twenty feet away, Austin suddenly sprang to his feet and began to back away in apparent fear. Instantly, Sasquatch let out a bellow and gave chase.

Austin was back-pedaling rapidly down the hallway. When the creature was nearly upon him, Austin suddenly reached out and grabbed both of Sasquatch's wrists, dropped to his back, slammed his feet into Bigfoot's stomach, and using the creature's intertia, flipped him over backward.

Sasquatch went flying over Austin's head, and landed on his back in the pile of rocks the technicians were working to clear. The creature let out a moan, temporarily stunned. Austin scrambled to his feet and tore down the hallway toward the ice tunnel.

He knew that his only ally was momentum, so he built up as much of it as possible. When he entered the ice tunnel, he was moving at better than forty miles per hour. A third of the way through the tunnel the sleep effect began to hit him. Immediately, he launched himself into the air, feet first. Austin hit the metal door and its outside camouflage of rock, like a locomotive running down a chicken coop. The door burst outward, its covering of rock spraying across the inside of the cave like grenade fragments.

Austin got to his feet, shook off the effects of the relatively small amount of the ice tunnel's effect that had time to get to him, and ran from the cave. The daylight was piercing, beautiful. He breathed in a gigantic lungful of mountain air, then ran off to catch Shalon.

Chapter Twenty-one

Trinity Base was nearly paralyzed with anticipation. Few of the men there had ever been within a hundred miles of a nuclear detonation, let alone felt the effects of one. Yet in two minutes and thirty-eight seconds they would do just that. First there would be a dull roar, then the ground would begin to shake—slowly at first, then more vehemently, until the birds fled the trees squawking out their fear.

Cups and saucers would rattle and some of them would fall off tables. At ground zero, the earth would bulge up a little, toppling older trees in a radius of several hundreds of yards, then the earth would fall back down, forming a slight depression which before the year was out would be covered with new vegetation. After the bomb would come the earthquake, and many of the effects of the bomb would be repeated. Finally, a section of land would be displaced slightly—perhaps only half an inch, but a whole area of North America would be saved from a major quake, at least for a time.

Oscar Goldman sat by the telemetry truck, his feet up on the edge of the work table. Next to him, Tom

Raintree monitored the countdown. Goldman had become, by then, quite numb. He was resolved to the idea of losing Austin, who was both his best friend and greatest achievement. And, though he despised himself for thinking such thoughts, he wondered what he would say to the President. That he had allowed six million dollars' worth of the taxpayers' money go running off into the forest in pursuit of a mythical monster named Bigfoot, never to be heard from again? Was that what he would tell the President? To die for a cause is one of mankind's oldest and most favored diversions. To die for no reason is the worst sort of folly. There would be no posthumous decorations, no Silver Star nor Medal of Honor, just another vacant apartment.

Tom Raintree flicked a switch and spoke into a PA microphone. "At my mark," he said, "two minutes and thirty seconds till detonation."

He flicked off the switch and turned his attention to Goldman.

"Oscar, can I get you anything? Some coffee?"

Goldman shook his head no, and didn't even bother to look at Raintree.

"I got a six-pack in the jeep." the Indian said.

"Later, maybe," Goldman said quietly.

"Look, Oscar...I'm sorry."

Goldman nodded.

"Look at it this way," the Indian said. "If Steve was anywhere in that area, he would have been found. There were hundreds of men out searching a relatively small area. No trace was found of him. To me, that means he's not in the area. Maybe he got lost, or maybe he's off in a House of Pancakes somewhere, having lunch."

"He would have called," Goldman said.

"How? When he left here, he didn't have any communications equipment."

Goldman smirked ironically. How do you explain to someone that your best friend has a radio transceiver built into his leg? He decided to stay silent, and let the subject drop itself. Steve Austin was dead. There was no other explanation.

Tom Raintree turned his attention back to the PA system. He checked the clock, switched on the system and cleared his throat.

"Two minutes to detonation," he said.

It wasn't hard for Austin to figure out that the underground nuclear explosion would be detonated at the same place where Marlene and Ivan Beckey were abducted. It was there that Ivan planted sensor 19, the only one that got the aliens excited. It was also the only site on the fault line close enough to the compound for an underground explosion to be a threat. So Austin made for it with all possible speed.

He didn't fear interference from behind. The aliens were sure to stay in the compound, and Bigfoot, assuming he wasn't seriously injured when Austin tossed him, was unable to match Austin's speed. Austin ran unimpeded, and before long found himself a position on the hill above the detonation site.

In the small clearing was an array of equipment

resembling a capped oil well more so than a bomb site. A fat pipe stuck three feet out of the ground. Atop it sat a large box containing the control equipment necessary to effect the detonation. The actual trigger was a radio signal from Trinity Base, but all the firing equipment was in the metal box atop the pipe.

Austin inspected the site using the zoom feature of his left eye, when scanned the nearby terrain. A hundred and fifty yards up another hill from the site was Shalon, who had also seen the detonation site and was running, albeit much more slowly than speeds of which Austin was capable. Immediately, Austin ran to head her off, to beat her to the equipment.

The time remaining until detonation was one minute and fifteen seconds. Shalon, using her Time Line Converter, got to the detonator in the wink of an eye. She pulled open the access panel and studied the wiring within the metal box. She traced wires, and finally found a pair of wires that particularly interested her. She ran her finger along them, and though she seemed to know what she wanted, perspiration stood out in pearl-sized beads upon her face. She peered into the deep recesses of the control box, and not satisfied by what she saw, moved quickly to the access port on the other side of the box and pulled it open. It was then that she heard the breaking of twigs, pushing aside of underbrush, and finally, heavy footfalls, and realized she was not alone. Instinctively, she knew who the intruder would be.

Austin was barreling right toward her at full

bionic speed. The sheer power of the man frightened her. It was one thing to measure it on a sophisticated electronic device kept within the security of the compound. It was quite another thing to watch that power coming at her, directed at her, in anger. Self-preservation overcame devotion to duty. She jumped away from the control box.

Austin stopped a half-dozen feet away.

"Leave me alone, Steve," she pleaded.

"Shalon—I can't let you stop this detonation."

"I *have* to," she said. She was nearly frantic.

"No," Austin said firmly. He dove toward her, but her hand flashed to her TLC, which was hooked onto her belt, and she was gone, to materialize closer to the detonator.

Something about the idea of diving for a woman and coming up only with air bothered him. Austin clambered to his feet and glared at the girl.

"Please, Steve—"

"No."

"I must stop it—to save my colony—my people."

"Before it was a compound. Now you're telling me it's a colony?"

"I mean...oh, never mind. What about my people?"

"What about *my* people?"

"I'm sorry," she said.

"That's wonderful," Austin said dryly. "Listen to me. The compound is important, but it's not worth the sacrifice of so many lives. Don't do it."

"I'm sorry," she said.

"I'm touched," he snapped, and dove for her. Her hand flicked down for the TLC, but Austin got her with a good tackle, knocking her backward onto the ground, just a few feet from the detonator.

He had one arm around her back, forcing one of her arms up, and he had her other arm grasped firmly in his hand. There was no way she could reach the Time Line Converter. She knew it, and howled like a caged leopard.

"No—let me go," she screamed.

Austin rolled on top of her. He pressed down with his head and held one of her arms in captivity while he made a lightninglike grab for the TLC. He snatched it from her belt and stuck it in the first convenient spot that came to mind—his mouth. Then he threw the girl over his shoulders like a sack of potatoes and started to run away from the detonation site. She continued to scream, but he paid no attention. She was securely pinned between his bionic arm and his shoulder, and had no means of escape.

Austin took her and ran for the high ground, if only because the underbrush was lightest in that direction. They were about two hundred yards upslope of the detonation site, when there was a deep, muffled explosion, a low, ominous rumbling, then suddenly the ground heaved upward beneath them. Austin was tossed completely off his feet and landed on his back, with the girl falling across his chest.

"No," she cried, "no."

The very earth itself was shaking, rising like a loaf of homemade bread. There was above them a mammoth flurry of leaves and birds. Austin struggled to his feet, only to be knocked down again. Finally, he stuck Shalon's Time Line Converter into a pocket, picked her up and continued as best he could up the slope. She was sobbing, unable to control herself, convinced that all her associates were dead.

After a few more seconds of running, the rumbling suddenly abated. Austin halted, still carrying the sobbing girl. "It's over," he said.

But as soon as he said it, he knew he was wrong. The explosion had ended. The earthquake was just beginning. Once again the ground began to shake, and Austin ended up on his back in a deep pile of leaves.

"The earthquake," he breathed.

Back at Trinity Base, Oscar Goldman greeted the arrival of the earthquake tremors by getting off his folding metal chair and sitting on the ground, his head buried in his hands.

"God help you, Steve," he whispered, as for the first time in a very long while, a tear curled down his cheek.

Chapter Twenty-two

Austin had made it to the timberline. Below the girl and him, the forest shook wildly. Using the infrared scanner, he could see a huge, circular section of land glowing with heat, not enough to start a fire, but sufficient heat to remind Austin of the awesome forces involved a short distance away.

Shalon stayed with him, her arm wrapped around his waist, totally dependent on him. Sometimes she would cry, sometimes just whimper. But whatever, it was a far cry from the cool, superscientific attitude she had held previously. Her dependency brought out even further Austin's like of being the protector. He scanned the horizon for danger and, when he looked up the relatively gentle slope of Battle Mountain, found it.

A rock cliff above them weakened, with pieces crumbling and falling down the slope to a spot near where Austin and the girl were standing. Suddenly the cliff let go in an avalanche of stone and dirt. Austin pulled Shalon beneath a small outcropping of stone and stood over her.

As the great rumbling in the earth continue, Battle

Mountain proceeded to shed loose bits of itself. Austin fended off several decent-sized boulders, three to four feet across, and split another in two.

"My people," Shalon cried pitifully, "my people."

In the underground complex, the aliens were feeling the full force of the earthquake. Chaos reigned everywhere. Machinery that was not tied down fell, and the crystalline walls shook, and in parts, shattered under the forces of the quake. Dust and slabs of stone tumbled from the ceiling. In the main corridor, Sasquatch stood stoically, fending off the stones as they fell around him. A man and a woman huddled close to him for protection. While in the large Council Chamber Room, Apploy and Faler struggled to maintain their balance as the compound was ravaged about them. The lighting had begun to flicker as soon as the first serious tremor struck. By then the lighting was switching on and off, and dimming and brightening, as if it had a will of its own. Finally the lighting flickered a last time and went out. Faler cried out, as if someone might be there to help him. If Austin were there, he might have said something about the wisdom of those who enter hostile territory without bringing with them a practical grasp of the ramifications of hostility.

Apploy huddled near a wall, hoping for protection. As he pressed his shoulder blades against the wall, a large section of stone cracked, separated from the stone surrounding it, and broke loose.

Apploy turned in time to see the hunk of granite falling down on him. He tried to protect himself, but he was no Steve Austin. The arm he held over his head snapped like a matchstick, and Apploy went onto his back on the floor of the chamber. A cascade of rocks fell upon him. He fell silent, without a sound, barely breathing.

Austin lowered his bionic arm and stole a cautious peek out from under the rocky outcropping that had helped shelter the girl and him. The dust was just settling, though large portions of the timberline still were obscured by debris. Austin blinked heavily as sunlight filtered through the dust and assaulted his eyes. He rose up slowly and looked for Shalon.

The girl sat beneath the outcropping of rock. Surrounded by rubble, she was staring off skyward, in a turmoil of emotion. Austin reached for her, but she pulled angrily away.

"Let me *alone*!" she yelled.

"Shalon..."

He pulled several large stones away from her.

"I want to help you," he said.

"To go where?" she said, desolated. "You may have succeeded in saving *your* people—but you've *buried mine*."

"Look," Austin said, "they may still be alive."

She looked at him with derision. Yet he still tried to convince her.

"There's still a chance," he said, "and if they are

alive they'll need our help."

He extended his hand to her.

"Will you come with me?" he asked.

"I'm afraid of what I'll find," the girl responded, an ugly image of death fixed securely in her mind.

"Could you live with yourself if you didn't try?" he asked.

Shalon looked at Austin and decided. She took his hand and allowed him to help her to her feet and brush the dirt from her clothing. Austin reached into his pocket and produced her Time Line Converter. He handed the device to her.

"Can you use that thing to keep up with me?" he asked.

"Yes."

"Okay, then," he said, "let's go."

He started to run, she touched a button on her TLC and together they moved at bionic speed in the direction of the cave/entrance to the underground compound. Austin led her to the cave into which he first saw Sasquatch disappear. She grasped tightly onto his arm and allowed him to lead her into the dark cave.

The cave was still thick with dust. The entrance to the compound stood open, evidence of Austin's ability to open any tin can even from the inside. The metal door was torn as if it were a World War II Liberty Ship on its way to the bottom of the North Atlantic.

"Did you do that?" Shalon asked, pointing at door.

"Yeah, twice, once coming and once going.

Doors have been my specialty, ever since I turned bionic. I've taken a heavy toll."

"I don't know how you can joke at a time like this."

"Yeah, well I don't know how you can pass yourselves off as being cultivated, benevolent and—what was the word Apploy used? Mature, that's it—mature. I don't know how you can pretend to be these things while you amuse yourselves by directing an eight-foot robot dressed up as an ape to snatch backpackers."

"You just don't understand."

"No, the problem is that I *do* understand. Regarding people as being tools is hardly a novel attitude on this planet. You call it science. We call it totalitarianism."

"I just can't talk to you," she complained.

"Tell me," Austin said, "how many have you lost?"

"What do you mean?"

"Come on—you must have lost one or two. How many people got a glimpse of Sasquatch and kicked the bucket?"

"Kicked the—?"

"Died, of a heart attack, while he was bringing them in to be tested."

The girl was silent, but her eyes turned in embarrassment toward the ground.

"That many, huh?" Austin said.

Still there was no reply.

"You see," Austin said, "that's the difference between us. You said you liked me, but were willing to sit back and watch lots of my people die. On the other hand, I don't like your attitudes one bit, but I'm still willing to save your lives."

Chapter Twenty-three

The ice tunnel was dark when Austin kicked aside a few rocks and ushered Shalon into it. There wasn't a trace of light, and no sound other than water dripping.

"I take it this thing is off," Austin said.

"It is," Shalon said. "The power chamber must be damaged. There's a compartment here someplace."

"I just want the lights turned on, not the sleep process," Austin growled.

The girl felt along one side of the tunnel until she found a section that pulled out. From it, she took a square lantern and switched it on.

With the lantern in front of them, Austin and Shalon moved quickly down the dark tunnel and into the rocky corridor in which Austin had had his most recent battle with Sasquatch. Rubble was everywhere, and near the pile of rocks Austin had brought down to seal the corridor, a man lay quietly, partially buried beneath rocks. Apparently, more rocks fell from the hole Austin had created during the tremor, trapping workers beneath it. Austin bent over the man and felt for a pulse.

"You *do* have pulses, don't you?" he asked.

She nodded. Austin stood and turned away. "He's gone," he said.

A few feet away, another technician was pinned beneath a long flat rock. Austin lifted the rock and pushed it to one side.

"Can you help him out?" he asked.

Shalon bent over the man and began examining him. He started to moan when she touched him.

"I think his leg is broken," she said. "He'll be all right. Come on."

She led Austin down the tunnel, over the pile of rocks, which technicians had largely cleared when the tremors began. They made their way to the Council Chamber, which was a shambles. The air was heavy with dust, and dimly burning emergency lights gave the room a deathly pallor. Near the remains of the shattered conference table, half buried beneath fallen rocks, Sasquatch was pushing against a gigantic building stone that had toppled and trapped a man beneath it.

The beast was pushing with all his might, but without moving the stone. Next to him, Faler watched in bewilderment.

Austin and the girl hurried into the room.

"It's Apploy," Faler said, pointing at the unconscious figure of the compound's leader underneath the stone.

"Is he alive?" the girl asked.

"Yes, but it's hopeless."

"Maybe not," Austin said. He stepped up beside

Sasquatch, who eyed him suspiciously. Austin braced himself and dug his shoulder into the rock. He began to push. Still Sasquatch just looked.

"Hey," Austin said, "it's you and me, kid."

Sasquatch watched Austin as he pushed against the stone. Then, with a little grunt, the creature joined him. Working together with their combined strength, the stone was slowly raised. Shalon helped Faler pull Apploy out from under it, then Austin and Sasquatch set the stone back down.

"He's still breathing," Shalon said. "Quick—the TLC."

Faler unhooked the device from Apploy's belt and handed it to the girl.

"What are you doing?" Austin asked.

"Adjusting his TLC slower," she replied. "I'll slow down his metabolism until we can operate."

Out in the main corridor, a long string of emergency lights flicked on, giving the corridor the same sickly pallor as the Council Chamber. It was a far cry from the ethereal brilliance of the compound's normal lighting. A young technician hurried into the chamber.

"Shalon!" he exclaimed, "we have several more badly injured."

"Can you save Apploy and the others?" Austin asked.

"I don't know," the girl responded. "We have the electromedical techniques, and the neotraxin compounds. But we have to get full power restored."

"Where's the power chamber you mentioned?"

"It's at the deepest level of the complex," she replied. "A thermal converter that uses the heated water from the volcanic vent to make electrical energy."

"The access tunnel has been sealed off," the technician said.

'See—I *told* you it was hopeless," Faler said.

"You never quit, do you?" Shalon snapped.

Faler shrugged.

"Where's that access tunnel?" Austin asked.

"Nobody could get through it," the technician said.

"Not even me and my friend?" Austin asked, cocking a thumb at Sasquatch.

"It's possible," the technician said. "It's possible."

"Come on. I'll show you," Shalon said. "Sasquatch." The girl led Austin and Sasquatch out of the Council Chamber and down the hall, while Faler trailed after them.

The access tunnel leading to the generating room was located a hundred yards below the main corridor, down a long series of tributary corridors and tunnels. The access tunnel was narrow and about eight feet high, and entirely blocked by a huge stone slab and a host of smaller boulders.

"This is it," the girl said.

Austin rubbed his hands together and walked up to the pile of debris.

"Better stand back," he warned.

Shalon and Faler flattened themselves against the wall while Austin and Sasquatch worked feverishly, at bionic speed, tossing rocks down the tunnel. Before long, they cleared out all but the large slab.

"This one is gonna be rough," Austin mumbled.

He put his shoulder against the rock, joined by Sasquatch, and the huge stone began to move. After pushing it a few inches, they paused.

"Come on," Austin said, "we can do it."

Again they tried, and again the slab moved a few inches. Several more tries, and the access tunnel was open wide enough for a man to squeeze through. Austin peered inside. Flashes of electrical energy illuminated his face from within the generating room, and the crackling sounds of electrical arcing assaulted the air. A loud hissing noise provided crude accompaniment, rather like an extremely large tea kettle that had been left on the fire too long. Shalon stuck her face into the breech provided by Austin and Sasquatch, and distress immediately registered upon it.

Inside was a mass of equipment clustered about a thick pipe leading down into the rock. Several red lights glared and flashed ominously. A thick electrical cable danced hideously, with sparks flying from the tip of it whenever it touched anything. And the large pipe leading down to the volcanic vent had ruptured, spewing steam across the room.

"You can't go in there," she said. "It's the main steam line from the volcanic vent. That steam is superheated."

"Then I'll have to be careful not to burn my fingers," Austin said, starting to squeeze through into the generating room.

"Steve," she said, in a frightened, little voice.

He looked back at her, winked and resumed squeezing through the opening, which was barely large enough to accommodate him. Inside the room, sparks flew while steam cascaded throughout, touching everything.

"Replace the cable first!" Shalon yelled. "The orange junction box."

Austin heard her instructions, looked around and spotted the box. Beneath it was a female plug into which the end of the flying cable normally fit. Austin stuck a finger of his bionic hand into the plug and cleaned out some shards of ripped conductor. Then he reached out with bionic speed and grabbed the end of the flying cable. Sparks danced up and down his bionic arm. He took the cable and shoved it back into its appointed place. Abruptly, the sparks died down, then disappeared entirely. The cable was secure.

Austin turned his attention to the steam pipe. He fought his way through the billowing, high-pressure steam to the pipe itself. He reached his bionic hand through the red-hot steam and tried to place it over the opening in the pipe, but the pressure of the escaping steam was enormous. It pushed his hand away.

Covered with moisture, both steam and sweat, Austin redoubled his efforts. Again he pushed his hand toward the rupture in the pipe, and with a supreme effort closed his hand over the hole. Steam spewed out from between his fingers. Austin slowly tightened his grip on the pipe, pulling the metal, squeezing it closed. Slowly but surely the driving steam diminished, then stopped entirely.

Austin backed away from the pipe, water dripping off every inch of him. He gave a glance at the cluster of control equipment located near the pipe. One by one, the red warning lights began to blink off.

Chapter Twenty-four

With full power restored, the medical examining room was again a center of intense activity. While Austin and several compound workers watched, Shalon inserted a hypodermic needle into a small vial of blue serum, drew out a portion, then handed the vial to an assistant. In the distant background, Sasquatch observed the proceedings expressionlessly.

"What do you think?" Austin asked, nodding at the prone form of Apploy, who was laid out on the same white table upon which Austin himself had spent so much time.

"He'll make it," she said. "The repairs to his legs were successful—"

She held up the needle and examined it.

"—and our neotraxin will ward off all disease and infection—as well as speed his recovery."

"He should've died from those wounds," Austin said.

"You should have died from yours," Shalon said. "You see—science does have its uses."

He smiled and watched as she injected Apploy

with neotraxin.

"It's really magic stuff, isn't it?" he said.

Shalon nodded and looked at Austin thoughtfully. Then she turned her patient over to an assistant.

"Keep a close eye on the ventricular," she said. The assistant nodded.

Shalon looked up at Austin for a moment.

"Are you ready to go back now?" she asked.

"I've got to," he said.

The girl nodded reluctantly.

"I—all of us—owe our lives to you. You shall not be forgotten."

Austin smiled.

"I wish I could say the same," he replied.

"You know we *must* erase your memory of us...and our compound here."

"I understand. But tell me, how does the erasing work?"

"A simple form of radiation. It's similar in many regards to X-rays, but has no harmful effects. We'll use it to erase your memory, going back to around the time when you first saw Sasquatch. With most persons, we leave a trace memory of Sasquatch, to discourage them from coming back or thinking about the experience too much. In your case, we'll erase back *before* you met Sasquatch. No sense in leaving you with any bad dreams."

"That's very thoughtful," Austin said.

A technician came over and grasped Austin's hand.

"Thank you for everything," he said.

Faler, seeing the man's action, joined him. "I

want to thank you, too,'' he said.

Austin grinned. ''I think you ought to go home.''

''I still do, too.''

''Why don't you?''

''It would take so long. We'd have to get a message off to home, then wait to be picked up. Six months at the outside.''

Shalon decided to interrupt. ''But we can't go,'' she said. ''Our mission isn't completed yet. We have three years to go.''

''It took you 250 of our years to get through the first two years of your mission,'' Austin said, ''do you mean to say that you'll be around for another couple of centuries—''

''I'm afraid so,'' Faler said.

''—grabbing people, scaring them out of their wits, and sticking them in test tubes?''

''It must be done,'' Shalon said.

Austin shrugged.

''Perhaps,'' he said, ''and perhaps not.''

He walked over to the reclining chair and sat down in it. A technician placed a flat electrode against the top of Austin's head. A bundle of cables ran from the electrode to the computer bank in the wall. The girl moved silently to the chair and waved the others away. Austin and she exchanged a lingering look. She took his hand, bent over and kissed him one final time. As she did so, she pressed a small vial of neotraxin into his palm. Austin wrapped his fingers around it and, at the first opportunity, slipped the vial into his shirt pocket.

''Good-bye, Steve Austin,'' she whispered. She

pulled back and the machine was switched on. There was a low hum, then Austin's eyes closed. A minute later, Shalon turned off the machine and removed the electrode from the top of Austin's head.

"Sasquatch," she said. The creature lumbered slowly to the chair, slipped his hands under Austin and lifted him. With Shalon watching, Sasquatch carried Austin out of the medical room, down the main corridor, and finally, down to the exit. The girl watched wistfully as Sasquatch, with Austin in his arms, disappeared down the ice tunnel.

Sasquatch laid Austin down gently in a clearing right near the timberline, stood and stared down at him for a moment, then lumbered back to the compound. As soon as the giant was gone, Austin opened his eyes, looked around him and stood up. He straightened his clothes and made a vain effort to spot the aliens' video sensor. He knew there was one someplace, and that they would be watching him from within the confines of the underground complex.

Austin was right. Shalon and Faler stood in front of the large, rectangular monitor on which they first spotted Steve Austin. Both of them were dumbstruck.

"What's going on?" Faler asked. "He shouldn't be conscious for another fifteen minutes at least."

"I know," the girl said grimly.

They watched as Austin turned in the general direction of the compound, reached into his shirt pocket, produced the vial of neotraxin, tossed it up into the air and caught it.

"I assume you're watching and can hear me," Austin said.

"He's talking to us," Faler exclaimed.

"I can see that," Shalon snapped.

"But how could he—he shouldn't remember a thing. And the equipment was working perfectly."

"You see," Austin explained, "I have this plate in my head which was designed to repair an injury and strengthen the skull. But it also does a pretty neat job of blocking X-rays—or any other rays like them."

Shalon shook her head in dismay.

"So your little memory eraser didn't work. Sorry to have to exit in such a sneaky fashion, but I really couldn't work up the strength to bust out one more time. Now that I'm safe, and away from you, I have a few things to say. One, give my regards to Sasquatch. Tell him I'm sorry we didn't meet under better circumstances. Two, I figure this vial of serum—"

"That's neotraxin," Faler explained. "He stole a vial of it." Shalon remained silent, declining to correct the misconception.

"—just about pays us back for two and a half centuries of being treated like guinea pigs. Maybe it will work on humans, maybe not. At least, it will be a lead for our medical researchers to follow."

"Third," Austin continued. "I'm going to go away now. I have work to do, and people that might miss me. But I'm coming back, in six months. If when I come back I don't find a big hole in the ground where that compound is, then I'm gonna assemble a couple of Army divisions and give you a little first hand field work on the subject of barbarism. I suggest that you simply leave. Call up your home and have them send a taxi, but be gone—in six months. In the meantime, I will make sure that this area is quarantined. There will be no further subjects for you to study."

Shalon sighed deeply and reached out to take Faler by the arm.

"Maybe it's for the best," she mused.

"Oh, and one other thing," Austin said, "check that steam pipe. The repair I made won't last more than a couple of days."

Shalon switched off the screen, and with her hand still coupled to Faler's arm, walked out of the room and down the hall. Out on the timberline, Austin, having completed his speech, turned and started to run casually back toward base camp.

Chapter Twenty-five

"That's an incredible story," Goldman said. "I mean, between the two of us we've come up with some pretty hairy stuff, but this one beats them all."

"It sure does," Austin agreed.

The two men sat on a knoll above Trinity Base, leaning against a medium-sized redwood. Their legs were stretched out on the soft earth, and between them sat a half-consumed six-pack of Coors.

Below, the last of the workers assigned to clean up the area was leaving. Tom Raintree sat in his jeep, warming up the engine and keeping a respectful distance so that Steve and Oscar would have time to talk. What had been Trinity Base was desolate, filled with tire tracks and littered with saplings cut down to make way for vehicles.

"Look at that, would you?" Austin said. "What a mess."

"It'll grow back. A year or two from now this place will have returned to the wild."

"I suppose so," Austin said, reaching into his shirt pocket, withdrawing the vial of neotraxin and dropping it into Goldman's palm.

"So that's it," Goldman said.

"Yeah. Remember that article you and I read a couple of weeks ago, about research into whether immunity to disease is genetically based?"

"I remember."

"Well, my guess is that this stuff works along those lines, influencing the body's DNA to produce a sort of general immunizing agent."

"We'll look into it," Goldman said, and put the vial in his pocket.

"I don't know if it will work on us," Austin said.

"We'll find out."

Austin got to his feet and finished his beer.

"We'd better get going," he said. "Tom is hot to get back to the lab and analyze the data from the San Andreas sensors."

"That should be some data," Goldman said. "The whole fault line jumped a quarter of an inch. Not jumped, actually, *slid* would be more like it. Damage was confined to a few broken windows."

"So the West Coast is safe for another couple of years," Austin said. "Do you think you'll be able to get this patch of woods sealed off for six months?"

"I can do it. I figure we'll use a cover story about Dutch Elm Disease, or disease-carrying ticks, or something in that line. Do you think they'll go?"

"Oh, they'll go," Austin said, stretching his arms. "They think we're savages, remember. Just by myself, I managed to put the fear of God into them. Now that they have the impression we're sending in the Army if they don't leave, they'll be on the next boat—bet on it."

Goldman climbed to his feet and picked up the beer. The two men walked slowly down toward the jeep. Tom Raintree revved the motor anxiously when he saw them coming.

"So Bigfoot is a robot," Goldman said. "Well . . . so much for legends."

"Yeah," Austin said, almost sadly, "so much for legends."